LETTERS TO HIM

Letters to Him

Not all goodbyes are permanent

by
Cheyenne Saunders

PITTSBURGH, PENNSYLVANIA 15238

RoseDog Books
585 Alpha Drive
Pittsburgh, PA 15238
Visit our website at www.rosedogbookstore.com

ISBN: 979-8-89027-445-8
eISBN: 979-8-89027-943-9

Prologue

One more kiss and I'll go.

I promise you, you'll never have to hear my voice again. Never see me again. I can't promise not to watch your life in pictures. Not to stare into the river of your brown eyes or swim in the depths of indentions of your cheek, or color roses with the shade of your lips. Your smile bites my heart in one of the most painful depths of despair I have ever sunken into.

I set down my pencil and take a deep breath. How do I write something like this? How am I expected by so many to say goodbye? To place something like this on his still chest, as he's dressed up all nicely in a suit and tie. Except that's the thing. That won't ever happen. He is already buried according to Mrs. Dean. My messages have gone green, he's gone, and I have to say goodbye to him. I have to let him go and be okay with it. My chest and nose light on fire at that thought. Tears stab at the rims of my eyes and warm, salty droplets leak out and spill off my chin. The page grays in a small circle beside, *goodbye*. Goodbye to you, not that you would have cared for me. You never wanted to really be mine. You wanted someone to love you, and God I did. You died. You killed me when you died, and you never even let me know if any of it was real. How could you do such a thing to a person? Maybe you are cruel. Were cruel. Now I mourn you but it's no different, I've cried many nights for you to want me back. I guess in a way, some sick way, I find solitude in this. In your being gone. Because now you can't break me anymore.

I pick up my pencil again, pointing the lead tip at the top corner of the lined paper. It scratches along the white sheet. I smile for the first time in a month.

Letter one.

Chapter One

I wonder what perfume everyone would pick to remind them of me if I died. If I crash my car or walk off a cliff. What scent would bring them comfort? Or would they even care enough to require it?

For him, I chose one that smells like a fire in the summer. Something about it makes me think of him. Of his smile and that feeling. I spray it on my shirt and grab my keys and bag heading for the door. It screams on its hinges as I push it open and lock it. A little girl sits playing on the steps to the fourth floor. I toss her a bag of goldfish crackers and she smiles happily. One foot after another until the bottom step trips me. That's truly my luck. I pull myself up and wipe the gravel from my palms. Collecting my things and unlocking my car.

The city bustles around me, noisy phone calls and clicking high heels, the streets in a dense sea of people—rushing to work, interviews, home, coffee shops, or to try their hand at acting. For me it's a quickened coffee shop on the corner, Beverley's Brews, cute name for a cute place, I guess. It's rustic-looking, with deep red brick walls and shelves of books that mostly collect dust. Except for the ones that I chose to take home every now and then. Beverly is an old, fragile lady; she makes the desserts in the back with her slew of college students working the busy counters. The shop is in between Times Square and Rockefeller. Lots and lots of business. It makes the hours pass at a quicker pace.

I push open the glass door lined with red. Vickey works at the register while Burke and Diane make the drinks and bag the baked goods. Vic lets out a puff of air when she sees me and smiles. I shove through the mob and slip under the counter because there are about ten cups of coffee sitting on the sliding panel. I rush to the lockers and pull on my black and gray apron. Then I rake my hair into a ponytail and throw my things into my locker running to aid Vic. I open the other register and start marking off drinks and food, handing them out to people and ringing up the stragglers that don't know what a line is. Before I know it, the closing shift is rolling in, relieving us of our sturdy stations so we can get to cleaning. Vic lets me go to the back to help Mrs. Bev.

I place at least seven pans in the ovens and mix some icing, placing fresh goods into the showcase glass and on the pillars outside the windows. With that I clock in my hours and gather my tips before exiting. I made about $430 in tips tonight; could be better, could be worse. Since there were four people working it was less. Bev's does great in tips, especially from out of towners. The rest of my day is spent shopping for random necessities with my tipping money and the rest goes to my rent. I finish up some work for my classes and settle in for the night.

My cat, Broome, hops up onto my bed curling up. I finally got to look at my phone.

Mom- I booked your ticket for next week, excited to see you!

I forgot about this honestly, which shows in my lack of packing. I haven't been home for a year. Ever since… he… left me, I couldn't bear to be in that town. Be back on the streets we walked across and see the shops he took me to. Especially the school and my room. I don't know how I am supposed to stand in my room after all this time knowing he isn't here anymore. But mom wants to see me for Christmas, I didn't even go home for my birthday like usual. I sigh and type back- can't wait. I can, I don't want to have all those reminders of love, or fake love.

Luckily, I at least had already told Bev I would be out of town for the week. Leaving with no presents and only $600 to my name. I should probably at least get Mom something, maybe dad if I ever see him. He'll work all week, knowing him, and all I can do is hope he doesn't show his face. Broome is going to stay with Vic and her fiancé while I'm gone. As much as I would love to take him with me, I have big plans for Mom's present this year. I hop up from my couch and grab my suitcase, then fold clothes and place them in along with toiletries. Then I grab my box. It's not big but not small. It can be hidden easily, and it holds my heart. It holds words I could no longer send to him, words that needed to be said. Some angry, some sad, but all of them I would scream in his face if I could. When he died, in a way, the person I was died with him. I immediately dyed my hair brown. Not the blonde that he would twirl around his fingers. However, I don't have the energy to keep up with it so it's almost completely back to blonde. I wear my glasses again. I changed myself because looking into the mirror broke my heart. I hate remembering him, so I do whatever I can to prevent that from happening.

Death is all around us, all the time. You read the papers and posts, see the funerals and graveyards. See tributes and dedications. But death has a funny way of creeping into your own life. I had only experienced it two other times. My grandma, who died of a heart attack, and my uncle who hung himself. I only went to my grandma's funeral, though. Uncle J never had one, he was just cremated and shipped to his mother. I never went to his funeral either. Looking back, maybe I should have. His brother texted me saying it would hurt their mother too much to see me cry. So, I stayed. I tunneled in on my classes and job and finally moved out of my dorm and into a lone studio apartment. You'd be amazed by how ambitious death can make you. Maybe I should thank you, Asher, but deep down the resentment I hold for the last words you typed before the crash.

Asher- I don't know how to love you.

I had no words. No reply. Later I texted you a paragraph expressing how deep my love for you was. How it drilled into my bones and paralyzed my heart. No reply. I won't lie, I hated you for that. That no reply. I longed for an, *I love you too*. But it never came. Instead, it was the call. The text. The deleted accounts and green bubbles. I love you never came. And I live with that fact every single day.

Chapter Two

Letter #97

A boy kissed me today. It was a petty one compared to how you used to. Truly it meant nothing. Absolutely nothing. I shouldn't have to ask for you to forgive me. You're dead, I accept that now and I can't keep pretending I mail these to you every time I write one. Do you remember Senior Night? You were all dirty in your uniform and your mom and brother walked with you across the field. I was still a Junior. All dressed up in my dance uniform clapping and cheering for you. You smiled at me. I was only your best friend, though. I'll never forget what you did that night....

"Go Asher!" I called. The rest of my team bounces around me while the cheerleaders do a random cheer. Asher lifts his hand, a smile plastered across his face. He looks at his mom, and she nods. As they go to read off his plans for the future, he looks over and hands the flowers to his mom, and then... he bolts. I stand still as gasps fill the bleachers. He jogs up to me, "What are you doing?" I whisper. "This." He snakes his arms around my waist and lifts me up over his shoulder, running back to the arch of balloons. He sits me down and his mom grabs my hand holding it tight. "Now my family is here, carry on."

That night was one of the best. My heart fluttered when you smiled, but... you never kissed me. You never laid your lips on mine, and when you drove me home, and wrapped the threads of my messy hair around your fingers, "beautiful" you said. I blushed. I begged you to kiss me once more. You laid your lips on my temple in a soft, second long moment of affection and you

*left. I went inside, my dad was livid. That night he threw me
down the stairs and locked me in my room. I don't want to know
what he would have done if our lips touched. But I would have
accepted it for one kiss from you. One that was long awaited.*
   love, Sabrina

You were mine. For a brief time. You could have swept up Carrie Galipsey. She was a senior, she was in cheer, she was gorgeous. But you chose me to stand beside you. My dad was never fond of anything I did, and if it gave him an excuse to bruise me, he did it. But at the end of the day, I can't be mad, you were mine. That was before it all became complicated. Before life mixed up all our emotions and dragged me down. I tuck away the letter and close the box, laying it on top of my clothes and zipping shut my suitcase. Might as well take all my thoughts about the memories we created.

When I crawl into that bed, all I can think about is you. All of you.

* * *

Broome is the culprit for me waking up as soon as the sun is spilling over the buildings. His water bowl is empty, even though it was over halfway filled last night. If you laid this cat in a puddle, he would soak up the water like a sponge. Still, I fill it and place it down, stroking his back as I lift back up. Today feels surreal, like the earth stopped turning in my mix of dreams about you. Tomorrow is the day I fly back into that place of nostalgia. I flip on the TV; some scary movie is what I need today. That and pizza. Pizza heals all. Broome and I curl up on the couch until the sun rises and falls, lining the tall buildings in an orange haze. I love sunsets, when they aren't bubbling in a boil of unhealthy heat.

Around eight, I pack up Broome's things and place him in a carrier for Vic. We head two streets over to her apartment and I ring the bell. "Visitor?" The speaker is staticky. I press the button, "Victoria Bay Apartment 2C," I say. The lock unlatches and I swing inside, heading to the elevator. Broome meows to me. "Just a second dude." The elevator stops two floors below Vic's, the doors open, and I look up. God, I wish that I didn't because this boy's smile seems like enough to make me forget what pain is.

"Evening." No. Not a voice like that too. I offer a small smile in return. We travel up and much to my dismay he steps off with me. "Not a peep, huh?"

I twist on my heels. "Who are you to comment on my decision to not participate in small talk?"

He chuckles. "Sam."

"Sabrina." I reach out and shake his hand.

"You're not very good at public interactions, huh?"

"I just chose to not get involved." He needs to stop looking at me. I'm going to faint.

"You don't live here. What are you doing in my hall?"

I lift the carrier. "My friend is babysitting this week."

"Christmas vacation?"

"You could say that."

"Hot date too?" Please dude, stop.

"I wish." He smirks, an evil one, one with bad intentions that I am not prepared for.

He opens his mouth to respond but to my rescue Vic opens her door, "Can you please give me my god-baby. I got him a new Harry Potter collar." I offer Sam a wave and duck behind her door.

"Thank God you exist," I sigh to Vic. She smiles and scoops Broome from his carrier. He snuggles into her. I think my cat loves her more than me.

"So, secret Sam, huh?" She wiggles her eyebrows in an annoying middle-school way.

"Secret Sam?" The name itself is cute in a way, like an inside joke I can now be a part of. "We've been neighbors for years, well, since I've lived here. He is quiet, and never talks to anyone. No one knows anything about him except his name."

"So, you and your three other neighbors took it upon yourself to create a character out of him?"

"In a way yes, but he kind of gave us the pathway to do that."

"Maybe he just doesn't want to talk to your annoying ass." I stick out my tongue and Vic does the same. We talked for a couple minutes then I finally headed home, collapsing into my bed.

* * *

My alarm screams at me around 4:00 a.m. God, why can't airplanes leave at a decent noon. My eyes stay stuck together while I stumble to get ready.

The Uber beeps and I lock up, dragging my suitcase along with me. Mom says there is a rental already for me at home, a fancy one too. Anything for her depressed daughter who hasn't been home in a lifetime. Boarding takes its time as normal, and before I know it, my breath catches. My hometown lies below in an encapsulated manner. Frozen in a constant look of *Friday Night Lights* and bonfires. A blanket of snow covers all the brick buildings and gravel drives. I exit the plane into the worn-out airport, scanning over the small groups looking for—

"Brina!" There she is. Arms fling round my shoulders, and I stumble backwards holding my suitcase for support.

"Hi, Alyssa." I hold her tight.

"I can't believe you're home. I'm so excited, your mom is so excited!" she squeals, pulling away, hands placed firmly on my arms.

"I'm so happy to see you, Lyss." I can't cry right now. Not in front of her. "Who else knows I'm in town?"

"No one but us and your mom, of course, your dad is off to work." I nod, happy with her response.

"That's good, I'm glad." She offers a sad smile and loops her arm through mine, walking me to her car.

Alyssa doesn't shut up the entire drive to my house. My cheek is pressed against the glass, watching the familiar streets pass by. Memories flood my heart in a sickening way that could make me puke all over Alyssa's car. But by the looks of the leather, she spent a pretty penny on it. We drive by the high school and round the corner onto my street. Houses pass in a blur and then my mom is pulling me from the car into a hug. "Oh, Brina, I can't believe how much you've grown. I've missed you." Mom's cheeks are soaked with tears as she digs her nose into my shoulder.

"Hiya, Mom." Alyssa pulls my suitcase into the house, and we all gather in the kitchen.

"Your room is the same. I washed the sheets and remade the bed for you. Your brother recently put Fire Sticks on all the TVs, so there's Netflix and stuff." She is rambling. She's nervous, I can tell.

"It's all perfect, Mom, I promise. Is he—"

"Your dad will be out of town all week, and when he comes back... I kicked him out."

"I'm so proud of you, Mom," I say and wrap her up in a hug.

"I just wanted you home, and I know he was no good. For me or you. I was just scared to be on my own. You and Deryl are all I have." She's crying again. I hate it when my mom cries. "Now go settle in. Deryl will be here around eight tonight. He's brought Christina and the kids." she smiles. I walk up to my room. Today is a lot more than I care for. I twist open the door and flip on the light. Pictures still line my mirror and I approach them. Alyssa and I were in our dance uniforms. Old birthday parties, including my Sweet 16. I wore a baby blue dress, with lace at the top and flowy satin to my knees. My hair was a curly mess and makeup half smeared from dancing. In this picture Alyssa stands holding my hand while Asher has his arms wrapped around my waist half lifting me up from behind. Our smiles blur together in the memory....

"Come on, it's time to sing!" Lyss calls. Asher smiles down at me and I go to step into the kitchen. He grabs my hand first, pulling me back to him.

"Ash, let go; they're going to start a riot if we aren't in there." He pulled me into the back hall, and I leaned against the wall.

"I wanted to give you your birthday present away from the crowd." He removes a black velvet pouch from his white button-down's front pocket.

"Asher...," I warn.

"Shh, open it." I carefully undo the strings and pull open the drawstring top.

"Asher this is—"

"No, don't, just open it, please." He's nervous, and it's making my heart race. I sigh and reach in, pulling out a gold chain. A gasp falls from my lips before I can stop it. On a dainty gold chain, a small sparkly A shimmers in the dim lamp lighting of the living room next to us.

"This must have been expensive; I can't accept this." He covers my lips with a finger and shakes his head, removing the necklace from my hands. My heart thumps in my chest as he leans into me, I move my hair and he clasps the latch shut around my neck. I can feel his breath on my shoulder, and it erupts my stomach in a mess of butterflies.

"Happy Birthday, Brina," he whispers, finally pulling back. His face is so close I can smell his cologne lingering. We sit staring for twenty heartbeats, as he leans in, I feel as if I may faint. But the itch to kiss him presses into me in a heart-stopping way. I can feel a graze of his lips—

"Come on it's—whoa." We break apart and stare at Alyssa, a smirk is plastered on her lips. "It's time to sing," she says and grabs our wrists.

~~~~~~~~

I realize I'm crying when the tears are drenching my shirt. That night, and so many nights like that I can't convince myself he is gone. That he may have never even actually loved me at all. I can't for the life of me think that it may have all been fake. Asher was always sweet before he graduated. You couldn't catch us apart. Taking my mind off things, I begin unpacking, putting things away in the same drawers that house tiny tank tops, and shorts too short for my body now. I grew up in New York according to my mother. She thought I was getting surgeries when I thought that the distance allowed change. As I place some shoes in the closet, my fingers brush the familiar velvet.

The memory seems unhinged when I pull the necklace out. I don't know how it got back in the pouch, nor why it was put neatly back in my closet. Last I saw it was flung across Ash's room. It was right before I left for college. He never told me goodbye. If there's any time to wear it, I assume this Christmas is it. I fasten it around my neck and place my hand against it. Letting the metal soak into my chest. This feels okay, maybe this week will be okay.

Dinner approaches and I walk downstairs to people bustling in through the door at a grand total of five. Ten years through two months in order, Eli, Ebony, Evan, Emmit, and little Evangeline. Deryl always wanted a giant family, luckily, he and Christina made that happen. Finally, I spot my older brother and rush over. He spins me around hugging tightly. "You're not seventeen anymore, Sis," he laughs, and I shake my head in response. The night is spent catching up. Lyssa leaves around ten when all the littles are sent to their blow-up beds in the playroom. I finally say good night and head to bed myself. Taking a long shower with all my teenage products, back when skin and hair care was a huge deal. I get to use candy cane-scented shampoo and sugar scrub on my legs. I exit feeling like a newborn baby. Sliding into some expensive pajamas that fit a bit too tight, before pulling myself under the covers. I settle in, turning on a movie and looking down at my phone.

Unknown- I just couldn't get you out of my head, asked 2c for your number, hope this isn't too weird –Sam :)
~~~~~~~~

Chapter Three

I'll have to make a mental note to personally strangle Vic as soon as I get home, considering she gave my personal phone number to a man I said three sentences to. Plus, thinking about him feels wrong. Especially while I'm here. His eyes bored into my soul; they reminded me of Asher, of his deep brown eyes that were so warm. Sam had those eyes, the inviting type that can make a girl forget her own name.

I don't want to think about a boy, a man. In this town at this time of year I'm pretty sure I could get imprisonment from it. Right now, I need to think of my mom, who just received her copy of divorce papers. Mom has her own car, the house is in her name, and Dad has given her a pretty settlement in return for no charges. I agreed to not fess up in a court that Daddy used to hit me so my mother can be taken care of. Not that she couldn't do that on her own. My mother is one of the strongest women I have ever met along with Mrs. Bev. They take care of themselves; that's how I want to be. I want to be my own person, pay for my own things, and not rely on another person. Therefore, I haven't sent Sam a message back yet.

"You're scared." Alyssa smirks.

"Am not."

"Is he hot?"

"Hotter than you." She reaches beside her and launches a pillow at my head.

"Seriously," she laughs "I haven't heard anything about your dating life since your high school sweetie," she says way too easily. I look down. "Have you not talked to him?" What does she mean by that?

I stare at her for a long time. "How would I?" She shrugs and looks down to her hands. That was just about as weird as a random guy texting me at midnight. I think she can tell I'm over the topic and switches up to Christmas.

"Your mom is going all out this year. She has been shopping since May."

"That isn't a surprise to me."

"She really missed you, pulled out the baby pictures every Thursday dinner."

"You still do those?"

"Of course, Anne is a better cook than my mom. Plus, I think she needs the company." I look up. Lyssa has gorgeous hazel eyes. I was always jealous growing up.

"I think I have a solution for that. I've been working on the best Christmas present ever." I smile.

Alyssa and I leave the house, climbing into my rental car. We go into the busier part of town, where a new mall sits. It's probably the newest thing in this town and recently renovated. We walk in, linking arms like we're shopping for prom dresses again.

"Where to first?" she asks.

"PetSmart" I answer. We veer into the store.

"Why are we here? Something for that kitty of yours?"

"No. Vic probably has bought Broome everything they're selling in these stores for Christmas."

"Why are we here?" I lead her into the dog aisle.

"Mom's Christmas present," I say with a wink.

I pick up a dog bed, collar and matching leash, toys, food, treats, and some puppy pads. "You're really getting her a puppy?" she asks.

"Yup. German Shepherd; she is fresh and ready for tomorrow." Lyssa stomps her feet rapidly like a five-year-old meeting a pony. I shake my head and we continue shopping until I feel as if my feet may just light on fire. I drop Lyssa off at her apartment and then hurry to the house to pick up Lola—Mom's new baby. I drive up a dirt road, lined with thick snow and ice. My poor little car tries to pull up the road and I eventually round the corner to come face-to-face with a beautiful farmhouse. Once the car is in park, I pick up my phone. Maybe Sam can be allowed. After all, what am I waiting for?

The cold pricks my skin while I walk up the porch, this place is gorgeous. I ring the bell once and blow into my hands trying to warm them up a bit. A swift breeze sweeps my coat, wrapping around me. My body jitters and I look up as the door clicks open. I look up and I can practically feel myself faint. How?

"Asher?"

God how is this happening? How could he possibly be here? My lungs tighten, razor-sharp barbed wire wrapping them up tight. *Breathe, Sabrina.*

You have to breathe, it's the only thing that's going to keep you from fainting. His eyes are locked on mine, react. Please react.

"Brina... you're—"

"You're alive?"

His eyes are full of sorrow, full of sadness. "I... uh, I'm—"

"I'm here for Lola." I cross my arms and look down. Questions flood my mind in a daze. A minute passes and he opens the door farther. I cautiously step in, it's even prettier on the inside. A couple beats later, a small puppy launches to me. I kneel and play with the sweet thing. She licks my face and I groan, wiping it away. "Her shot papers and stuff are all in this folder," Asher says.

I can't react right away. "You're dead. You're supposed to be dead," I say, mostly to myself.

"Sabrina...."

I stand straight. "You died! You died! Your mom called me, your brother texted! Do they know you're—"

He reaches for me, and I stumble back. My wet boot slips and I fall back against the wall. The weight and reality set in. Like a black crushing wave of pain hitting me in the face.

"Calm down Brina, please—"

My breathing is uneven, fast. I can't catch my breath. It won't stop. Please God get him out of here. My pain bubbles up in my chest. I can't get it out. I claw at my face and hair until there's no other option. A scream rips through my body like a demon has possessed me. His hand touches my knee, and I jerk back, hitting my head on the wall, another scream crawling out of my lips. Little Lola is huddled in a pile of shoes.

I scream until black spots poke around my eyes. This, this is the same feeling as when I got the call that he died. And now he is standing in front of me. My face is buried in my knees as I try and even my breathing. His voice registers again, and it keeps my chest tight. "Sabrina, breathe."

I look up, face burning. "What did you do, Asher?" He looks guilty, good.

"I-I don't even know. I thought it would be best. For you, for me. It wasn't meant to go so far, I swear, Brina." He lays a hand on mine atop my knee.

"You died."

"No, I didn't."

"A plane crash—"

"Never happened."

"There was a funeral."

"There wasn't."

"Your mom never posted anything about you." I can't understand.

"I asked her not to, ever again. I was done hurting you and everyone else. I needed a new start in life."

I stand quickly, faltering a bit. "The money is here," I say and toss an envelope down to him. Grabbing Lola's leash, folder, and small going-home bag. I run. He chases me as I practically dive into the car. I drive quickly, probably unsafely, arriving at my house right as Mom starts the Christmas Eve festivities. Before I go in, I gather myself, tying a big purple bow on Lola. I hush her and place her in a box. She does rather good, considering I bribed her with a treat. Deryl greets me, gathering the hint gifts for Mom from the back and hastily placing them in gift bags.

The house is warm when we enter, offering comfort to the most surreal experience of my life. Everyone sits to open the gifts from family before Santa comes tonight. Mom goes first, against her will, of course. She is confused as she opens the extensive amount of dog items. Landing on a beautifully made collar Lyssa picked out a tag engraved with Lola. I put the box on Mom's lap, and she hesitantly lifts the lid. Tears prick her eyes as Lola pops up and licks her nose. She smells like his house…. Mom begins crying and lifts the puppy out of the box. All the kids gather to meet the newest addition. Deryl nods at me, we did good. Now she won't be so lonely. We continue opening presents until I can't keep my swollen eyes open. Everyone says good night and I go to my room, locking the door. I climb into bed and pull out my box. I need something….

Letter #40

Bev's was a mess today, Ash. Really it felt like all of NYC was here. Christmas really riles them all up. I miss Christmases with you… I miss your gag gifts and you and Deryl pranking each other. Things really do change.

"Ash, please hurry; it's so cold." I cringe. He tugs hard at the Christmas lights and dusts off his hands. "He's going to kill you," I groan.

"I think this is my best work, Brina," he laughs loudly. Christmas lights cover my brother's car on top of a thick layer of plastic

wrap. He is going to strangle Asher for this one. "Come here," he says, motioning for me. I stumble over to him through the snow, pressing myself to him, soaking in any warmth he may have. He rubs my back softly and kisses the top of my hat. "This thing is so stupid," he laughs and flicks my pom-pom.

"Is not," I pout. Our eyes lock and I sigh, breath freezing in the air.

"You're beautiful, Sabrina." This is the first heat I've felt in hours and it's spreading across my face like wildfire. He leans down, brushing my lips with his. Please....

When you pressed your lips to mine, I knew I loved you. More than one person should be able to. I could have stood out there, numb feet and all, as long as you wanted just for that kiss. I was encapsulated by you and that feeling. I'd do anything for that feeling again... I miss you so much. Merry Christmas, Asher.

Love, Sabrina

That Asher would have never hurt me like this. A sob scratches up my throat and I end up crying until I can't keep my eyes open anymore.

* * *

The kids wake up the entire house at five sharp. My eyes are stuck together and sore. I rub them trying to loosen the gunk, but it does nothing. There's a knock at my door and then Deryl's voice,

"Brina, you okay."

"My eyes won't open," I mumble. If I cry again, it'll only be worse.

"What do you mean, let me see." He flips on a light and I flinch. "Jesus, Bri."

He walks into my bathroom, and I hear the tap, moments later he is next to me, rubbing my eyes gently with a warm washcloth. They loosen and I finally open them. "Did you know Asher was alive?" He looks confused.

"Yes, obviously." How did this happen...?

Then it hits me. I never said anything. To everyone, I cut off from them all. I shake my head and push away, we walk downstairs, and the kids bust down and see all of Santa's presents. I smile at them, so excited. Before I can redirect myself, I pull out my phone. Typing, **come to Maine.**

I've gone crazy.

Chapter Four

I feel like the day after Christmas is the slowest in the entire year. Everyone decides to clearance shop, clean, play with new things, or sleep. Tough one… sleep. My body is melted into my sheets until three in the afternoon when Alyssa decides to launch her body on mine.

"Why haven't you called? I wanted to show you my new stuff," she pouts.

I groan under her, "People who want sleep." She flops off me and I lift up, grimacing at the sting in my chest. "Lyssa. I love you with my entire soul, but the idea of me being in your room watching you play with makeup over being asleep is… well, you know."

Alyssa leans back against an oversized pillow. "What did you get?" She nods to me.

"Books."

"Just books?"

"And some clothes, makeup stuff, stuff for Broome, and house stuff," I list. Mom really did her best to get everyone exactly what they wanted. Alyssa talks more about her new makeup, and I grab my phone, eyes widening at the initial message.

Sam- Anything for a date with you, where to, gorgeous?

Me- Castine

Sam- Don't tease, I have a plane for work, I will be there by tonight

This is obviously a very bad idea, but then I remember what happened yesterday; *see you then.*

* * *

She won, she drug me out of my pajamas and warm bed right into a cold coffee place that smells like old bread. "I saw Asher."

Her eyes snap away from the bitter, badly made coffee. "How is he?"

"Not dead." This really catches her attention.

"What…?"

"Asher's mother and brother told me he died. His accounts were deleted, he disappeared, and I believed it."

"That makes no sense. How did you buy it?"

"I never talked about him. I cut everyone off, all of you in this town. His mother was crying, his brother too. I don't know what I was supposed to think."

She slumps back into her chair. "Wow." She's in a daze, and I can understand why; it's the same one I've been in. Asher deserves an Oscar; this is by far the most obscure thing to ever happen to me. "So, he really made you think he was gone? That's so cruel, though, especially for Asher." All I can do is nod in return; I wonder if this is shock. I have never had any situations that resulted in shock. Not even a car wreck if you can believe that. "I'm going to beat him up," Alyssa finally says.

"Yeah, because you're so tough."

I look up and my eyes bounce to the door, right now my life feels like a cruel joke. Asher walks in, a woman close behind. "Oh God." I cringe and slump into my hoodie.

"Oh no, do you think we can sneak out?" Alyssa asks.

"Maybe." I'd rather die. She packs our stuff quickly and grabs my wrist, our hoods are on our heads, and I angle my nose to the ground. Our amazing plan is ruined when my glasses slip off my nose, I bite my tongue and reach down to retrieve them.

"Brina?" Fuck. Alyssa and I stand up straight, hastily pulling the hoods from our heads, we must look so stupid.

"Hi." Lyssa smiles as fake as possible.

The woman holds tight to Asher's hand, melting into him in the most sickening way possible. "I didn't expect this," he says, scratching the back of his neck.

"Of course not, trust me I never expected to see you again." I knock into his shoulder walking to the door.

"What she said," Lyssa fakes a mic drop and runs to me. "That was the weirdest thing I have ever encountered, Bri."

I feel like I'm running to the car. "Trust me, the idea of having a ghost ex is pretty weird to me too."

"Sabrina, wait!" Nope. I twist around. Asher is rounding the corner.

"Alyssa start the car, hurry!" We dive into our seats, and she peels from the parking lot. Asher stops running, dropping his head to his chest. What's funny is I almost feel sorry for him, but what he has done to me and put me through feels illegal. I think it might be illegal to fake your own death. Maybe that's something I can Google when I get home.

"Can we still eat somewhere? It's dark and I'm hungry," Lyssa pouts. All I can do is nod in return. We just spent about twenty bucks in that smelly shop on soggy sandwiches and I myself am starved as well, but my budget is tight. I can maybe get out with a stomachache. Alyssa and I ended up in another diner, luckily this one is warm and smells like coffee. Lyssa splits her sandwich and chips with me, and we sit together for a long while. Asher and I were good. All our lives from five years old to now. Well, not now, to the end of my senior year, though. I never thought there could be anyone else for me. He was all I wanted and needed for forever.

Sam- Where to now?

There's no way. *Rally Diner.*

We sit a bit longer and the bell chimes breaking my daze. Sam is actually here, standing in between booths, hands shoved in his jacket pockets. "Oh God," I mutter.

"What?" Alyssa questions, looking up at me. I stand up, Lyssa watching closely as I walk to Sam.

"Hey, gorgeous." God that smile might murder me. "Why are you here?"

"I said I was going to—"

"Yeah, but we're not all that close to New York; this is a rather pricey trip just for a date."

"Ah, yes… well, Vic said you were going home for Christmas. My parents are in Hawaii. I have a connection for a rather cheap plane, and plus it gives me a chance to check up on business outside of New York." He makes no sense to me.

I slump my shoulders. "This way."

Alyssa perks up when he approaches the table. "Wow, are all the girls here this beautiful?" She blushes a deep red and I scoot into the booth, him beside me.

"Who's this?" Alyssa asks. *Here we go.*

"I'm Sam. I live in her friend's apartment building."

"So, why are you here?" She is going to play twenty questions.

"To see Sabrina."

"Why?"

"Because she keeps me up at night." This is what makes me make eye contact with him.

"Hm," Alyssa hums, leaning back into the booth.

"We need to go Alyssa," I say.

"Can I come with; I haven't found a hotel." Why did the universe do this to me? Mom does have a guest room, maybe one night wouldn't do too much damage. If Vic felt he was safe enough for my number, I'll assume he isn't a serial killer. At least not a well-known one, and if I die, I better have a book written about me because my life has become the most bizarre plotline ever.

"Don't kill my family."

He holds two fingers to his forehead. "Scouts honor." *Asshole.*

Chapter Five

"Who is this?" my mother questions before we even fully enter the house. Deryl walks up beside her, crossing his arms over his chest.

"Sam meet Anne, Anne meet Sam. He doesn't have anywhere to stay. I offered the guest room," I explain to her.

"Is he a serial killer?" Deryl pipes in.

"I don't think so, but my judgment has been way off lately," I answer and move between the two of them, swinging Sam's duffel bag up the steps. It thumps on about the seventh step up.

"No bed sharing," Mom says, scowling. "It's nice to meet you, Sam." She offers a smile to him. I don't blame her. It would be hard to not smile at that face. He takes her hand in his and kisses her knuckles. She swoons and is suddenly under his spell as well. I have to give him some credit. He's good at this. Alyssa hollers a good night and runs out into the snow.

"This way."

We hurry up the steps, my need to be a good host is gone as I slip past his duffel, not bothering to lift the 100-pound thing again. He follows behind me while I lead him into the guest room.

"Nice house," he says while shutting the door.

"Careful. Mom might chop you up for that."

"Nah, she likes me." He winks.

"You're kind of full of yourself, aren't you?"

"Not in the least bit. I'm just confident this won't be my last time here."

"We haven't even had a conversation, Sam."

"We are. Right now. This counts as a pretty good one, lengthy too. I'm not really the talking type, though." I step away from him. He's dangerous for me, for my heart. But then again, I have seemed to be incredibly off on determining how men will end up. Sam seems decent enough. He must have a nice job to afford an apartment like that on his own. Vic works two jobs along with her fiancé's venturous occupation as an accountant. Not anything cool or fancy to him; he's still sweet and good for her. He balances her crazy in a way.

I sit on the bed while Sam sorts his things out, not fully unpacking but enough so I can see he brought boxers with tiny little candy canes on them. I can feel myself smiling behind the pure cringe of the situation.

"Like them?" He is awfully cocky.

"Hardly." I stand up. "We can go on that date, but tomorrow you need to make sure you find a hotel." I move to the door. "Showers in there." I jump over into my room, locking my door. I don't feel unsafe around Sam. That's part of the problem, though. He's a stranger and already feels like someone who should be here, who should be in my life. The idea of having another guy in my life that isn't a cat is probably the scariest thing about it. I haven't had anyone since Asher. I grab my box from under the bed and pick one out....

Letter #3

I got a cat. You hated cats, I guess I understood why from your viewpoint. Not everyone gets attacked at the ripe age of seven but somehow you managed to. You knew Buttercup hated kids. I don't know why you wanted to pet her. I still remember you crying. The summer heat had us both spilling sweat when we ran into my house.

"What happened to you?" Mom gasps, running out of the kitchen. "Buttercup got him, Mama," I say, holding on to Asher's hand while he cries. His entire chest was bloody and clawed up, teeth marks lined the side of his neck to shoulder. Mom hurries with a wet cloth and an armful of medical stuff. Some white bandages and a brown bottle of the bubbly stuff. I hold on to him while she wipes all the cuts and bites, dumping the bubbly stuff on them. He cringes into my arm, and I squeeze tighter on his hand. When Mom is done, she exits to call Asher's mom.

"Does it hurt?" I ask, slipping onto the floor in front of him. I lay my head on my hands on top of one of his knees.

"Not as bad as before. It just burns." He picks up the end of my ponytail, fiddling with the hair.

"Can I help?" I hate it when he's hurt; it makes me feel hurt.

"Just sit with me, Bri. Stay here." I sit up beside him on the couch again, resting my head on his shoulder. "I love you, Bri."

I hold his hand still. "I love you, Ash."

Asher, I think you are my other half. A soulmate, twin flame, whatever. You're something to me, though. Something important. I still can't believe you're gone. And you left me here, alone. At least I have a cat now, though, I guess. I named him Broome; Buttercup was too traumatic.

Love, Sabrina

I brush the tears from my cheeks and walk over to my collage of pictures. Pulling off all the ones that hold Asher in them. From five to nineteen, he was right there. How am I supposed to move on? Maybe I could if he was actually gone. I could convince myself it's what he'd want and force a date or two. But now knowing he's here, breathing. It complicates everything. Maybe it shouldn't. Asher wanted to no longer exist, at least to me. And by the looks of it, he moved on. That girl was basically eating him with her eyes. I know that Sam can be something good, but I swear, no man will ever hurt me how Asher has.

* * *

There's a knock on my door, I glance over to my digital clock. It's not a bad wakeup time, 10:23, I got to sleep in a bit. I stretch out my limbs groaning as they pop and unlock from their sleeping positions. Another knock sounds and I walk over to the door, grimacing at the icy cold of the wood floors beneath me. I whip open the door to see Sam smiling at me.

"Be ready by seven. I'm going to head out and grab a hotel," he says. I almost forgot about the date. "Cute shorts," he adds before walking away. I look down and cringe at what I'm wearing. The T-shirt isn't bad. It's loose fitting and meets just the top of my belly button, the shorts, however. They are tiny, from probably sophomore year, blue and fuzzy with tiny polar bears covering them. I don't even want to look in the mirror, the idea of however my hair might look now would only add to my trauma. Lola pops around the corner and slips into my room, hopping on to the bed. I swing the door shut and go into my bathroom, unwrapping my hair from its monster bun before I jump into the shower. Mom must have finally realized how cold it was in here because the heats kicked on by the time I walk over to the closet. I don't officially leave for quite a while, so I text Alyssa to bring some dresses and I pull on the same shirt as before and a pair of black leggings.

I'm only ten minutes into my show when Lyssa busts my door down, hangers piled into her arms and she launches the ball onto my bed, covering Lola. The puppy stays put, sleeping the day away beneath the heap of colors and sparkles. "I didn't mean your whole closet"

"This? You think this is my whole closet?" She begins laughing, so hard tears can be spotted at the corner of her eyes.

"Point taken, I guess." I lift one of the dresses. It's yellow, with white sparkles making a star on the hip with a dangerously high slit up the leg. "Alyssa."

"I wore that to my first ever party, the one with Carrie G. and Brad W. I swear you were there, I thought you were—"

"That was when Asher and I had that fight." I can't hear his name anymore.

"Well, not first-date worthy," she says, discarding the all-too happy yellow dress. She pulls and tugs from the pile, chewing on the inside of her cheek until she has four dresses laid out neatly beside me. "Try them on."

I scoop up the fabrics and walk to the door of my closet, slipping inside and turning on the light. The first dress is a deep blue, it's velvet and sleeveless, stopping just above my knee. It hugs my body a little too tightly for a dinner date. When I open the door, she immediately shakes her head. "Too sexy for a first date." I nod and go back in. The next is black and covered in sequins. It looks like a freshman homecoming dress. "No too—"

"Itchy," I cut her off. Number three is a green color, like a dark forest. It's pretty, silky, tight at the top and flows down to my knees, with long sleeves. Alyssa gives a thumbs-up for this one and I head in for the last. I'm most scared of this one. It's a medium shade of red. A similar style to the last but with only one long sleeve and the other side leaves my shoulder bare. There's some lace details on the sleeve and I'm in awe at the beauty of it. When I exit, Lyss gasps and hops up rushing to me.

"This one is the one. It's perfect, Brina." She's so excited and it reflects off me. This will be a good day and date because Sam is a good guy. He's cute, he's funny and sweet, he's… he's good.

Alyssa pins my hair up in curls so they'll be bouncy. She paints my nails and does my makeup and sits with me while I shave. Winter is no joke on my legs. Pretty soon it's 6:45. My stomach twists with nerves, while I pull the gorgeous dress on again. My hair is pinned on one side, and I put in my contacts, ditching my glasses on my nightstand. Lyssa matched my lipstick to the dress and put me in beautiful black strappy heels.

"You look perfect," she squeals. I check myself over one more time before the bell rings. She races down the stairs while I hide behind the wall.

"Good evening, Alyssa," he says to her.

"And to you too Sam," she replies in a British accent. I can't help but giggle.

"Is she ready?"

"Oh, you bet. Sabrina!" I twist around onto the steps, locking eyes with Sam. He's in a black button down and some nice-looking jeans. His mouth drops open and spreads into a giant smile. I grip on to the railing as I walk down, praying my shoes won't ruin this moment and send me flying down the stairs. Mom, Deryl, and Christina stand in the doorway to the living room,

"You guys are ridiculous." Sam takes my hand and kisses the top of it, lingering there a bit longer than he did with Mom's.

"Okay run, before Deryl kills him!" Alyssa says, shoving us out the door. I stop and turn to her.

"Thank you."

"Hush, go have fun," she says and kisses my cheek, shoving me out the door before slamming it. I step down with Sam and he leads me to a rather nice car. "Rental companies here are pretty great," he says, opening the door for me. I climb in and adjust my dress around me. I feel slightly overdressed for whatever he may have planned.

"Where are we going?" I question.

"I found this really good Italian place, it's about twenty minutes from here." He looks good driving, too good for me especially. I stare down at my hands, twisting my bracelet around over and over. He must've noticed because he slips his hand into mine easily. Like it's the most natural thing he has ever done. I push anything involving Asher from my mind and focus on this.

"What do you do for a living?" I ask.

"I work with a publishing company. I'm the guy that reads all the books and edits the good ones. What about you?"

"I'm in NYC for schooling. I want to be an architect. I draw up designs all the time. I love it. I love history and the beauty places can hold. While I'm at school, though, I work at Bev's with Vic."

"She mentioned that, and said you were good too."

"It's hard to be bad at a café, honestly. I show up and do my job. It's simple."

"True but people have an awful work ethic nowadays."

He's not wrong on that front. A lot of eager kids apply to Bev's, we hire them, and they end up quitting within a month. Work just isn't cut out for everyone, I guess, especially school kids. We arrived at the restaurant after sitting in silence. I've been to this place before. Asher brought me here when he—

Never mind.

We get seated next to the window that looks over a beautiful lake, the trees and ceiling are covered in white twinkling lights and snow surrounds the path and water outside. "What to drink?" He's a young waiter, probably eighteen, if I had to guess.

"White wine for her and water for me," Sam says, the boy nods, scribbling on his notepad before hurrying away.

"How do you know I didn't want water too?"

"Because wine tends to help girls relax a bit on dates." He smiles. He isn't wrong, although I wouldn't completely know if it wasn't for Alyssa. "Are you going to move back here after college?" he asks.

"No. This town is too heavy. And small, no place for my work either."

"You're too big for this type of town, Sabrina." The waiter comes back, placing down our drinks and a basket of bread. We order the special and he hurries away again. I sip my wine and set it down.

"There's not too big or small for this town, just functional and non, and I am non," I say to him. He tilts his head to the side and grabs a piece of bread, tearing it open and handing me the other half. I pick it apart, eating some. It's very good for plain bread.

"Are you going to stay in New York, then?"

I think for a second, the thought hasn't really been brought up. I still have two years of school left. "Maybe" I finally answer. "I haven't really thought about it, the location is ideal for work, though." He nods in return, the waiter finally brings the food, and we pick around the chicken and pasta. It's probably one of the best things I've eaten in a while.

Once we finish, he pays and we exit. "What now?" I ask. He grabs my hand and pulls me down the snowy path to the lake. The cold pricks my skin and I shiver against my jacket. "It's beautiful here," I say, and he turns me to him.

"You're beautiful."

"Oh eww, cheese!" I say and slap his chest. He laughs, and I can feel it in my bones basically. My hand is still on his chest, and he reaches up to hold it there.

"You're ridiculous, Sabrina," he says. I step closer to him, soaking in his warmth. These are not good lake shoes; the heels have sunken into frozen mud. "Sabrina?" I hum in response. "Can I kiss you?" I search his eyes for any hint of bad, any hint that will tell me not to. But I can't find any. I straighten up as he leans down and I press my lips to his. For the first time since Asher, my insides light on fire. It's hard to believe this is only the third person in my lifetime that I've ever kissed—that or sad. But Sam feels like I'm finally kissing someone good again. His arms are wrapped around my waist, and I've nestled myself in a position where his thick coat warms me up more than my own.

We break apart and he rests his head on mine. "You're something else, Sabrina," he says. I giggle a bit, and he goes to move to the car, but my feet are sunken in.

"Sam?" I call. He turns and laughs when he notices. He bends down and unclips the ankle piece, standing straight up again, he hooks his arms behind my knees and back and lifts me right out of my shoes. I laugh and wrap my arms around his neck. He carries me to the car, placing me in, and then runs to retrieve my shoes. This is a happy feeling, a good one. One I didn't know if I would ever get back again. And it's almost completely ruined when I see Asher standing in the doorway of the restaurant.

"You ready?" Sam asks while he slips into the car. My eyes are fixed straight ahead, where Asher stands staring right at me. His breathing is labored, and fists clenched at his sides. I break my gaze away from him and turn towards Sam, leaning across the console I kiss him again. His hand reaches up beside me and cradles my face.

"Let's go," I say when we finally break away. Asher is still staring at me; he doesn't break eyesight until the same bubbly brunette nearly knocks him over. He peers down at her and turns around, his hand in hers, before entering the restaurant. Sam backs out of the dirt lot and rests his hand on my thigh as we drive.

"Who was that?" he asks. I was hoping he maybe wasn't paying attention to what was happening.

"Asher."

"Boyfriend?"

"Hardly." The word gets caught in my throat, and I turn to face the window, resting my hand over Sam's.

"Should I be worried?" He sounds nervous, like he's about to lose me.

"Never." I smile and lean over onto his shoulder.

"I'm glad you rode my elevator," he says. As odd as it is, I am too. I'm glad for a lot of things right now. The only thing ruining what could be so good is Asher. This whole trip was supposed to help me overcome his death, well, not technically I didn't want to come. But I had hope that it might. Now all I have is a feeling, one that has made me feel almost completely numb to everything. Sam pulls into my driveway and walks me to the door.

"I had fun, but this is as far as I'll go," he says, holding my hands.

"Such a gentleman."

"I don't want your brother or mother to castrate me." He smiles, and I can't help but laugh.

"Good night, Sam."

"Good night, Sabrina." He leans in and kisses me one last time, wrapping his arms around me. I almost forget that numb feeling. We break apart and I unlock the door slipping inside. My back is pressed to the wood, and I blow out all the cold air in my lungs, inhaling the warmth.

"Fun night?" My heart stops and I spin towards the living room.

"Deryl what are you doing?"

He pushes off the wall and walks over to me, pulling my coat off and hanging it. "Why didn't he come in?" I rip my heels off and grimace at the feeling in my feet.

"You and Mom scared him, plus he's trying to be a gentleman," I say and move towards the kitchen. The fridge is full of leftovers from Christmas, but my eyes are scanning for Mom's brownies.

"Asher was never a gentleman. You two almost made Mom soundproof the walls." I slam shut the fridge and toss the plastic container on the counter, hard.

"Don't talk about him," I warn and grab one of the paper plates, cutting out a large brownie and tossing it into the microwave.

"Why?"

"Because, D, right now I could live my whole life without ever hearing his name again."

"But you were both so good together, you were so close." I grip the counter until my knuckles are drained of color. "He's engaged now ya know."

I look up, meeting Deryl's pitiful gaze. "And?" The microwave beeps and I twist around transferring the brownie into a bowl and popping some vanilla ice cream on it.

"She's a nice enough girl, bit of a poodle, though." He laughs at his own joke. I try to ignore him and smother the sugary snack in chocolate syrup. "Bri?"

"What?" I can't look up, if I do, he'll know I'm about to cry.

"What happened?" I sigh and sink onto a bar stool by the counter.

"He died, D." My voice is shaking when I tell him.

"Is that a metaphor?"

"No, he died. He deleted all his accounts, changed his number, his mom called me and his brother. They said not to come, that seeing me would make it worse."

"Is that why you stopped calling?" I nod slowly, looking up to meet his eyes. They are full of emotion. Full of anger, sadness, pity, all of it. "I never mentioned it, never posted it, I thought I was doing it for his mom. I guess I—" A sob breaks through. "I just needed him to disappear." He moves over and wraps an arm around my shoulders letting me fall into him.

"So, he pretended to die?" I nod in return, wiping my eyes with the heel of my hand. "What an ass." Deryl always makes things better. He pretends to not let this new knowledge get to him, but I can practically feel the heat of his anger radiating from him.

I find strength to pull away and grab my dessert, we say good night before heading upstairs. If I cry tonight, I'm letting him win. I'm letting him hurt me, when right now I want to be excited, I want to feel happy about the amazing date I just went on. So, instead of crying I turn on *Gilmore Girls* and change into my pajamas with long fuzzy pink pants and one of Deryl's large shirts. I snuggle into bed after removing my makeup and eat my brownie creation. I am done allowing Asher to control my whole life. I'm done being his little victim.

Chapter Six

The next morning, I make the decision to lay in bed all day with my curtains closed. Sam has texted and we have messaged back and forth a bit. He leaves for New York in two days, and I still have five days before I leave again. We have another date planned tomorrow, but luckily, I have avoided any and all plans so that today I don't have to walk on my sore feet. I hope he doesn't expect heels tomorrow, but he said that it's casual, just some lunch. It's close to noon by now and I sit up in the bed, pulling my box from under the bed. I sift through the letters and pull one out. I don't know why I want to do this, but it feels like I need to.

Letter #14

I danced in the rain in the middle of Central Park today with my friend from work, Vic, and I thought about you. I remember you loved the rain so much. I didn't like the storms. They reminded me of when my dad was angry. When he was slamming cabinets and stomping through the house. But you made the rain fun....

"Asher, come on you're going to get sick," I call out, shivering into the pillar on my porch. He's soaked and jogging up to me. I squint through the tough water droplets as he snakes his hand into mine, still standing in the downpour. "Dance with me, Bri." He smiles. I shake my head trying to pull away, but he holds tight to my hand. "Please?" he says and reaches into his pocket, upping the volume to the speaker through his phone. He jerks me forward and I scream as the cold water floods over me, drenching my clothes. He wraps his arms around my waist and drags me into the middle of the road, placing me back on my feet.

"Asher!" He smiles and places his hand on my hip and the other in my hand, dancing me over the concrete like when we were five in classes. He spins me off my feet and I wrap my legs around him, dipping back so the rain hits my face. Thunder booms around us and I face Asher again. He has the biggest smile on his face. "I think you're the prettiest person on the planet, Brina," he says. I smile and lean down, kissing him lightly. He starts spinning again and my legs unlock from around him, swinging in a circle while we kiss.

We ended up with horrible colds after that. Both bedridden for a week. But it was so worth it. It was magical to me. The rain, the thunder, the music, but most of all you. I miss that magical feeling. I miss you.

Love, Sabrina

I fold up the paper and put it back into the box. I almost forgot about that one. Looking at it now, though, I don't know how I could ever manage that. I enjoy the rain now, for the most part. In New York I would always have to remind myself that Dad was nowhere near me. He didn't have an apartment building, or number, or even phone number. But it's hard to just forget everything he put me through. No father should ever treat a child that way. Induced so much fear, I had to lock at least four different locks to feel safe. Back then Asher was my safety net. He was all I had to fall on. Deryl tried, but it wasn't the same. Dad went easy on him. His proud son with the perfect grades and life.

I tried so hard for my dad. I took all college classes to put myself ahead. I got perfect grades, and attendance even after what happened. I was the Dance team's captain in only tenth grade. I was home on time, I did my chores, and had a job to support myself. And still, he hated me. More than Mom who he said always took money from him, more than his own father who constantly put him in the hospital. Dad never liked me, but I always loved him.

I angrily wipe the tears from my eyes and stand up, stretching my sore muscles and popping my back. My feet are covered with warm socks, and I slip downstairs and throw myself between my mom and brother, laying my head on Mom's lap and feet on Deryl. "Hibernating?" Mom asks, taking a sip of her coffee. I nod firmly and twist to see what they're watching, same thing I was. Deryl has always had a crush on Rory. I wonder if he still does or maybe he thinks it'd be creepy now. Considering she was young in the show at least. I'm going to miss this when I leave for home, granted now I won't be as alone. Sam has brought out so much joy in me. Joy I was sure Asher killed. When the sky turns dark my family slips up to their rooms, hiding away for the night. I stay curled up to the corner of the couch, Lola nuzzled into my ankles. I'd say it was a pretty good lazy day. A knock sounds through the house, rapid and heavy. I wait to see if any movement happens upstairs, nothing.

The knock sounds again this time heavier, echoing through the sleeping house and I jump to my feet. Staring through the peephole my heart almost stops. I swing open the door to a heavily drunk Asher. He's holding the doorframe and slumping forward. "What are you doing here?" I question as he falls toward me, almost knocking me down. I steady him, helping him to sit on the bench by the door.

"I had to see you," he slurs, head looming forward. I stand against the door, staring, arms crossed over my chest.

"You shouldn't be here, Asher." It comes out as more of a whisper. He looks up to me, eyes red and puffy with tears running down to the corners of his mouth.

"I had to see you." He pushes himself off the bench and stumbles to me, pinning me against the door.

"Go home. I'll call you a cab, but you can't be here." I try to push him back a bit. The smell of stale beer lingers on his lips making me gag. He leans in, full body weight resting on me, and he rests his head on my shoulder. I try to push again, but he clings tighter. His shoulders begin to shake, and I can feel the thin cotton on my shirt soaking to my skin. I cringe. How is he crying? Why does he get to cry?

"Asher…." I push again, and he finally steps away, letting his body swing in anger while he twists to the wall.

"God, Sabrina, can't you hear me? I had to see you. You had to come back; everything was perfect! It was all going right because you were gone! I needed you gone! And you had to come back and ruin everything! Why do you ruin everything!" He punches the wall and I shiver down into the corner by the door.

I'm right back to when Dad yelled. When he threw me down the stairs and slammed my head into the kitchen counter. I shake and hide in myself while Asher moves to me dropping down to his knees. His hands grip my shoulders, and he drags me up with him holding me in place.

"I needed you to let go of me. I needed to live, and you ruined it! You ruined it all! How am I supposed to love someone else while you're here and I have to look at you again." My stomach is twisted into knots, tears slip down my face, and I turn so I don't have to look at him. I can't look at this person, whoever it is. Because this is not Asher. This is not my Asher. A sob chokes out while his fingers dig deeper into my arms, when he hears it, he steps back, letting me go. I slide back down the door and he stomps off into the kitchen. Deryl is looking down the steps and I push myself back up, holding a finger to his lips.

"Are you okay?" he mouths, and I nod, tiptoeing into the kitchen behind Asher. He stands with his hands gripping on to the counter, so tight his knuckles are ghostly white. I can't tell if he is crying again or just breathing hard.

"Ash…," I whisper. He needs to snap out of it. The last thing I want is the cops showing up to my house this late at night and the entire town telling Mom about what's happening. He heard me, I know, but he doesn't respond. Instead, he grabs a wine glass for the drying rack and throws it as hard as possible at the floor, shattering it in front of my feet. I can feel the glass dancing over my bare skin, and I jump back only to feel a piece crunch under my heel. The pain shoots up to my ankle and I fall back against the floor sliding backwards. He picks up another glass and slams it against the cabinets. Now Deryl is behind him, pulling his arms behind his back. "Asher," he repeats. *Asher, Asher, Asher.*

I watch Asher fall to his knees and sob. While my brother holds him. I dig the glass from my foot, tossing it on the floor and it bounces away from me, and I crawl over to him, kneeling right in front of him. His chin is to his chest, brown hair hanging in front of his eyes. "Ash," I whisper again. He looks up, I put a hand to his face while he focuses. Deryl's let go of his arms, and he lunges forward pulling me to him.

"I'm so sorry," he cries, hugging me. I feel it now. I feel all the pain. I feel my lungs and throat lit on fire. I feel the sinking weight attached to my heart. I feel how much I loved Asher Dean, and how much he loved me. The only thing was he never loved me like I wanted him to. Like I needed him to. I finally wrap my arms around his shoulders and hug him. So tight my arms feel numb. My face is buried into his shoulder, breathing in that scent. Summer fire.

Deryl has slipped away and started to sweep up the glass, but I can't manage to pull away from him. He's holding on to me as tightly as I was him. If I let go, I'm scared I'll never get to touch him again. I hear the steps creak while Deryl goes back to his room. We are both crying, my nails are dug into his shirt. Asher, this is Asher. This is my Asher. He loosens his grip and I unwillingly do too. We're sitting close, and I stare into his eyes, those eyes again. Those eyes I loved.

"Bri…," he whispers. I can feel his words fan my face.

I take a deep breath, "Ash." He places his hand on my cheek and I lean into it, accepting this feeling for a minute again. He leans in and when he kisses me it all floods back, like a tsunami. Knocking me down and taking me over.

We melt together like we used to; I feel like I'm going to faint from this feeling. This mix of pain. Of love. Of Asher. Asher. We break away, breathing heavy and labored. My mind flies, but just as it comes, any joy from this fizzles, and I quickly stand and back away.

"This was a bad idea; I'm going to get you an Uber. Or cab, or bus, I don't care."

"Bri, wait!" He scrambles to his feet and is planted right behind me. "Please."

"There is no please in this, Asher. You don't get to beg me. You get to plead; you get to fall to your knees and sob an apology because, Asher, what you have done to me is criminal." My anger boils in me, deep in my bones like a fire. My whole body is tensed up and I need to let this go. Before I think I twist on my heel and slap him, hard. It echoes through the house, ringing in my ears and I stand shocked, hand still raised. It stings, but I really don't mind it at this point. He deserved it, I can't even try to feel bad. When his eyes meet mine, I cringe with fear that they will resemble my dad's. Instead, they are filled with sorrow, tears pool and he squeezes them shut, holding his cheek with his hand.

"I am so sorry, Sabrina," he mutters. He leans forward and kisses my forehead before exiting the house. I stand shocked, my head aches trying to process this whole thing. I can't wrap my head around any of it. It all feels made up.

"Sis?" Deryl breaks my daze and I turn to face him. My insides feel like they're being sliced open, looking at my older brother with those sad eyes breaks me. My heart is ripped out and I can't breathe. I fall to my knees; he runs to me and wraps me in a hug.

"It's okay, Bri," he whispers. A sob rips out of my throat, so hard I can't even catch my breath. I can't breathe. I can't, I don't know what to do. What to think or feel. Deryl rubs my back and tries to calm me down. But I can't breathe. I gasp in; it feels like my lungs are tied tight with barbed wire. Mom's here now, with Christina. Both kneeling. Eventually, I go backwards, everything is fuzzy and black spots fill my vision. I can't breathe, I can't breathe; I can't feel, silence.

* * *

I woke up just in time for Sam and my date the next day. I didn't put on any makeup. Instead I dressed up in a cute sweater dress with some wooly tights and heeled boots. I slide into his car easily and he greets me by kissing my cheek. "Hiya, gorgeous." He smiles. I fight to return it, but my body aches beneath my clothes.

Asher left a few bruises where he grabbed me. Not to mention my heart feels like it's been torn up. I feel broken, more broken than when he died. Maybe it's because this time he hurt me, and I mean physically harmed me. That's not the Asher I knew. Whoever this person is, I want nothing to do with him. Not anymore. Goodbye, Asher Dean.

Chapter Seven

I get off the plane and search around for Vic and Sam, spotting a large sign covered in glitter reading "Welcome Home, Brina!" I laugh and make my way to them. Sam sweeps me up into his arms into a tight hug. I like that he came with Vic to meet me. It shows that he genuinely cares about me and about us. New York is colder than home was. I shiver within my coat and hurry to Sam's car.

Being home feels like a weight has been removed from my whole body, I don't need to worry every three seconds anymore. Besides everything else that happened, I'm happy to have gotten to spend time with my family again. We head to meet Vic's fiancé, Matt, first to pick up Broome, and then all go to my apartment. I unpack and we end up all piled on my couch watching scary movies. Vickey and Matt are cuddled up and fast asleep.

"I'm glad we're back in my regular territory." Sam smiles.

"Why's that?"

"So I don't have to review ten different places to take you on dates."

"You reviewed places?"

"I couldn't take you somewhere shitty and impress you, could I?"

"You never know." I laugh and he leans in and plants his lips on mine. I melt into his touch and before I know it I am straddling him. I pull back. "We can't."

"Why not?" he asks and kisses me again.

"I don't want this to start with just sex. I want this to be real. I need it to be."

"He considers me for a moment. "It will be." That's all I needed. I lay my head on his shoulder and slip off into sleep.

Chapter Eight

"Hold your breath!" Sam yells right before him and Vic's fiancé Matt dive under me and Vic and launch us into the air. Our screams blend right before we dip below the water. I push myself back up to the surface and find Sam, splashing water into his face.

"You're such an ass," I laugh, and he swims to me, wrapping his arms around my back. I hold tight to his neck, letting him swim in circles with me.

"I didn't want to get my hair wet." I can't help but smile. As much as I wanted to avoid the dry, knotted mess pool water creates, at least I'm having fun again.

"Where do y'all want to eat?" Matt calls. Vic is sitting on the pool's edge now, feet kicking at Matt while he pinches at her legs. I look down at Sam and shrug.

"Burgers sound good," he answers. I love burgers. It's what he cooked the week we got back to New York, it's what he cooked when he asked me to be his. I lean down and press my lips to his. He smiles into it, making me melt in his arms. Under this sun in the cool water. The moment is ruined when he holds tight with one arm and plugs my nose with the other before dragging us both under the water. When we stand back up, I wipe my eyes and slap at his chest until he lets me go. I can feel his brown eyes boring into me while I pull myself out of the water. The water drips off me, sending a chill down my spine as Vic hands a towel to me. I twist on the concrete to face Sam. His eyes rake over my body, and I blush against the fluffy white towel.

Matt slaps Sam on the back of the head before dragging him out of the pool, "Undress her later, I'm going to die of hunger." I bury my face in the towel, fully mortified now. This bikini is probably the most exposed I've been with Sam in our whole three-month relationship. It's not that I haven't wanted to, and he definitely has wanted to. I just don't want something fast and basic. I want love, as cringy as that is. And with Sam I feel like I'm figuring out how to love someone again. We pull on our clothes. My suit soaks through my jean shorts and loose T-shirt. We walk away from the pool and along the busy street until we find a diner. This one's not packed with people basking in the new April air. The boys battle for a booth against a group of college boys without shirts.

"Are you going to tell him about everything?" Vic asks, nudging my shoulder.

I turn to her. "Soon." She means everything. Everything about Asher and my dad, all of it. It's just that there's a mess of things that I don't want out yet. That I don't want to ruin that boy's beautiful smile. Not yet. The boys win their argument over the booth and usher for us to sit. I stand on my tiptoes and peck his lips before sliding into the booth. A pretty waitress skates to us and takes down our orders. I can't help but watch Sam as he watches her. His eyes scan hers and cascade down her body, if I don't sleep with him soon I think this might get worse. She leaves and Sam turns to me, but I slump back against the booth. He talks to Matt and Vic about something involving the new landlord to their complex.

The waitress returns. She hands out drinks. Sam watches. She smiles, Sam smiles. She grazes his hand with hers. I cringe. And feel a foot tap mine. I break my eyes away and meet Vic's.

"His girlfriend's right here, sweetie. Can we get a new waitress?" she asks. The girl falters. She finally looks up at me and offers a sad smile before leaving.

"Little harsh, Vic," Sam says and sips his Coke. I want to puke all over this table. But I don't, instead I scoot a little closer to the wall, and face the picture. It's an old fat guy in front of a little shed-looking place. I can feel the pressure of a sob in my throat, but I push it down. I won't cry; it's my own fault. "You okay?" Sam whispers. I bring my shoulder up to my ear and rub away his voice. He places his hand on my thigh and I flinch.

"Go ask *Betsy* how she is," I snap and move my leg away. He considers me for a moment, but is interrupted by a male waiter placing our food in front of us. Everyone digs in and I nibble on the unnaturally large burger. This group hang really needs to end, luckily Matt and Vic know how to read a room and leave us at my apartment. Sam picks up Brooke and sits on the couch while I move around to pick up the mess I left this morning.

"Talk to me, Sabrina," he says, walking to me. I huff and bend to pick up a towel and empty bottle of sunscreen.

"About what?"

"Earlier?"

"Nothing to talk about, Sam." I sigh and move past him into my bedroom.

"Come on, I'm sorry. I didn't mean to, I know that sounds stupid, but I didn't."

"You control your actions," I say and pull off my damp clothes. I throw them into the hamper and bend down to my dresser. Digging out pajamas. "Sabrina—" he starts.

"Don't, okay you were looking at her. She was looking back. I mean hell, you should have just asked for her number." I untie the strings to my bikini and twist to face him.

"Sabrina—"

"Really you're free. If you want to be free, then—"

"Sabrina, you're naked," he says. I stop in my tracks. Pajamas swaying in hand, wet bathing suit on the carpet and I look down. Shit.

I cover my body the best I can, and he stands, walking to me. I look down at my feet, my red nail polish has chipped. He hooks his finger under my chin and forces me to look at him. "I don't want Betsy. I was being polite. And I was also thinking about how cute you'd be with that uniform on. Not that this isn't"—he steps back and scans over my body—"beautiful, Sabrina. You're breathtaking." I bite my lip and look back down. He steps closer and kisses the side of my head. I look up and he kisses me, wrapping his arms around my bare hips. I let him kiss me like he wants me. His lips move from mine to my jaw, trailing to my neck. I clamp my pajamas to my chest harder and keep my other hand against his chest. He tries to step back, towards my bed, but I pull away.

"Wait, we need to talk first," I say. He looks disappointed but nods anyway and walks to my bed, sitting. I quickly pull on the clothes and join him.

"This is about that guy, isn't it?" he asks. I nod and lean over, pulling my box out. I can tell he doesn't really want to hear about this. But if he wants to sleep with me I need him to know it. All of it. "This is a box of letters. I wrote them when I thought Asher died. I want you to pick one. You can read it and know what they are. Then I'm going to tell you about the other stuff." He nods and reaches into the box, pulling one of the letters out.

Letter #58

I hate you, Asher. I hope you know that, wherever you may be. I was going through boxes today and I pulled out my old pillow-cases. Those light gray satin ones? I loved those. But right now I hate them....

"This is such a bad idea," I giggle as he slips through my window. He lands on his feet, biting his lip.

"I think this is a perfect idea." He bends down and kisses my cheek. I try to hide my blush, but he notices anyway and pinches my cheek. He moves past me, pulling off his shoes before launching onto my bed. I uncross my arms and walk over to my bedroom door, locking it, before sitting beside him.

"Turn the TV up," he says, poking me.

"You don't even like the Gilmore Girls," I say and he shrugs. I turn up the volume anyway, leaning back into my pillows. He moves so he's closer to me. He lays his head by my neck and plants little kisses down from my ear to collar bone. I pretend to not be affected. I keep my eyes straight ahead. He reaches for my hand that's crossed over my stomach and pulls me so I face him.

*"You're so pretty," he says and kisses me hard. I melt into him, I melt because he's Asher. God, I love Asher. He hovers over me and pulls at my loose shirt. I let him. He pulls off my shorts. I let him. He unclips my bra and takes off my underwear, leaving me completely bare. I let him. Everything he did I let him. I let him. I give up my virginity to Asher Dean. It felt like every part of me was on fire. His hands run up and down my body; he's possessive. He covers my chest in bruises left by his lips and covers my mouth with his hand. Finally he stiffens over me, I feel like my body might dissolve into my mattress. Asher rolls off of me and stares up. There are little glow stars still stuck up there from when I was five. They glow a light manila color against the gold hue of my lamp. I turn to see what Asher is doing, his back is to me, but I can still see his phone. **Lindsey- What are you doing babe?***

I cried for hours. You didn't pay any attention. I cried all of the mascara and eyeliner I had tediously put on for you onto my favorite gray pillowcase. When you fell asleep I went to the bathroom and sat in the hot water of the shower. My tears blended with the water and I cried until my vision was full of black spots. I hate these pillowcases. Just like I hated you that night.

Love, Sabrina

Sam stares at me, face solid and unmoving. I wait. *Don't hate me, Sam. Please don't.* He takes the letter back from me and folds it before placing it back into the box. "I'm not that lying bastard, Sabrina." he says and tackles me to the bed. He shoves the box off my bed and plants his lips firmly against mine. I moan against him despite the slew of secrets I still need to confess. But instead I give in. Asher and I did it a lot more after that night, because he wanted me. In that way at least. Now, a few years later, a new man is in my bed and I'm letting him touch me the way I never thought I would again. His hands are smooth unlike how… no. His hands are smooth, and new.

His kisses are hard and assertive, maybe because he just read about the loss of my virginity and wants to make this better. I smile into him, I melt into him. He pulls off my loose half-put-on pajamas hastily and pulls away long enough to remove his own shirt.

"I won't hurt you," he whispers, kissing down my neck and chest. I feel the foreign feeling of fire in my stomach, making me pull my thighs tightly together. This seems to appeal to Sam and he pushes my legs open with his knee. "Is this okay?"

"It's perfect, don't stop," I breathe. Honestly, I don't know if I'm ready for this, however the little purple thing from Walmart is nothing compared to a human experience.

"I want to be right for you."

"You are," I say and pull his shoulders up so that his lips meet mine again. He is still in swim trunks, thin, swim trunks. He presses against me and I wrap my legs around his back.

I'm definitely not ready for this, but I want so badly to be. I don't know if I should stop him. Stop this. I can't stop this. Not now; he is all worked up now. So I give in. I push his shorts down without fully breaking away. He works with his hands in more places than just my hips and eventually I need it. I need to feel Sam, and I'm sick of letting the past ruin a perfectly good future. But the past sticks with me, I close my eyes and suddenly Sam is Asher. Suddenly he is in me, moving with such perfection I'm not even sure it can count as human. His hands move over my skin and all I can feel are how Asher's felt the following nights after our first encounter. Focus, Sabrina. Maybe it's that I haven't been touched since I was nineteen, but I moan into his mouth, and scream through the apartment like I never could with Ash. I try to push any thoughts about my neighbors' well-being out of my mind. I'll handle the noise complaint later.

He wraps his hand in my hair, pulling lightly at the strands creating a dull ache in my scalp, exposing the base of my neck, he begins to kiss down my jaw, moving his way down my neck. My body tightens at the memory of Asher doing the same. He's devouring me in the most perfectly beautiful way, and yet I'm stuck comparing. Asher over me, his eyes and lips and movements. All of it rough, unlike Sam's soft motions. It comes in flashes between the two. Sam begins to shake above me and I use my legs to hold him to me. I want to feel this, all of this, and all of him.

He does one last thrust and drops on top of me. Both our chests rise and fall at a rapid pace and I can feel the buckets worth of sweat between us. He rolls off and I cuddle into his side.

"That was amazing, Brina," he gasps.

I smile and snuggle into his chest. "You're pretty great too," I mumble. I bite my lip and twist so I can look at him. His cheeks are flushed and eyes heavy. Soon enough he slips off into sleep and I gently remove myself from his grasp to use the bathroom. I find a button-up of his hanging off the towel rack in the bathroom and put it on. I didn't really get to eat earlier so I head to the kitchen. There isn't a lot to work with. Some chicken, noodles, and luckily enough sparse items to create a sauce. I cook the chicken and noodles, making a white sauce with some garlic, cheese, and broth. I'm mixing it all together when I feel arms wrap around my waist. His chin rests on my shoulder.

"My little chef," he says. I smile and twist to face him.

"I'm no chef, but I'm starving and I figured you might have worked up an appetite," I say and reach up to give him a quick kiss.

"I'm happy I met you," he says before walking to the table and taking a seat.

"I still had more to tell you," I say, bringing two bowls over to the table. He waves his hand at me. "Another day, please."

I just nod. I don't know if he will still love me after he finds out.

Chapter Nine

Sam and I have hit a spot where we wonder what's the next step in our relationship. He wants me to move in with him specifically. It isn't an absurd idea, it just makes it all feel even more real. We sit by the pool at his apartment complex, he's swimming around and I lay on the edge with a fluffy towel under me.

"You love the pool, can we add that to the pro-con list?" he asks, swimming to me.

"I guess so, but con, water makes winter colder." He grabs on to my arm and leg and pulls me in, water gushes up into my nose and I pull myself back up. He laughs so hard you couldn't tell who really got the air washed out of them. "Con," I cough. "You're a dick." His laughter continues while I climb back out and throw myself onto a chair.

"You love me; stop denying me, Bri. Just move in. It's closer to your work and school," he says and rests his chin on his hands.

"I guess we can try it," I give in. He has all the points. It would save me money, save travel time as well. We are serious now, so it feels like the only path for us to take.

Next thing I know I'm standing in the hallway of the complex next to Vic as the boys carry boxes into his place. I'm holding Broome, this whole thing has made him clingy. Sam had to fight a bit with the landlord to allow my poor cat to move in too. No Broome, no Brina.

"That's the last of it," Matt says, wiping his hands.

"Thanks for the help," I say and move to where Sam stands in the door.

"Welcome home," he says and moves me into my new living space. I set down Broome and he pads off into the kitchen, no doubt looking for food.

"Let me start unpacking and we can order in," I say and walk towards the kitchen. Sam agreed to let me keep a good portion of my stuff. I put up the plates and such before moving into the bedroom. He bought a bigger dresser and cleared three fourths of the closet. Considerate. He comes in about an hour later.

"Chinese is on the way." I offer a nod and continue setting up my bookshelf, wishing they hadn't taken it apart. "I'm happy you're here, Brina," he says and kisses the top of my head. I can't deny anything for Sam. Sam has made me feel alive again. But right now, knowing I have nowhere to go if things get bad, feels suffocating. Broome appears next to me and rubs his head on Sam's leg. I smile at that. I smile because Asher would never let a cat touch him. Broome has saved my life on multiple occasions.

"We can do this, right?" I ask while Sam sits beside me, holding Broome.

"Of course we can."

"No bullshit?"

"None," he says, bumping into my shoulder.

"Okay, let's get this built then."

I would rather jump off this complex than ever rebuild a damn bookcase again. Honest. We ate dinner and now I'm sitting in the living room while he sleeps in the bedroom. Maybe he wanted me here just so he could have Netflix and Hulu. I wouldn't really blame him, though. I'd do the same thing. Mom pays for them both, so I wouldn't go out to parties all the time. Pretty good deal for me. Honestly, I'd rather sit on the couch and watch TV anyway. While I watch some horror movie I'm sorting through a couple boxes, organizing them so they will be easier to put away later. My hand brushes over the familiar box and I pull it out. I haven't looked in here since Sam read that letter. I haven't even thought about reading one. I look around the apartment, one wouldn't hurt.

Letter #69

I got sick today because I remembered you. Not you in general. You'll never believe who walked into the shop today. Brittany. Remember? Brittany Jones, the one who had you crying for about four months. Gad, that period of time was awful. It was before sex was introduced between us, so it wasn't hard for me to console you. I helped you, restored the person that was stripped away. I built you back up... and then....

"You're a worthless, entitled, waste of air!" I shudder away from him while he slams another beer bottle against the counter.

"I'm sorry, Daddy!" I cry, but he doesn't listen. He stomps up to me and slams the broken glass against my head. Pain shoots through my skull like a knife. Warmth runs down my forehead. I touch the stream and stare at the red stain. I twist around and use all my strength to get to the door. His hand wraps around the bottom of my old T-shirt and I pull against him, gripping on to the doorknob. I finally rip it open and pull with all my weight away from him. I hear the shirt rip against his hand before I run out into the chilly fall night. My bare feet tear against the gravel and I run. Like a crazy person through the neighborhood.

"Asher!" I yell. I step up into his driveway and as soon as I reach the door it swings open. He meets me halfway and lets me fall into him. As soon as we hit the ground I cry. I cry so hard I feel like my throat is full of razor blades.

"What did he do to you?" he whispers. The only light on us illuminates from the street lamps, yet I can see that his gray sweats are now covered in blood.

"Asher?" a high-pitched voice asks. I push myself up and my eyes meet the green ones of Brittany. "You have to be kidding me!" I cry.

"Bri," he says, trying to grab me, but I just rip away and run again. My feet are raw and torn up from the rough terrain beneath them. But with the mix of pain from my dad's hard hands and Asher's betrayal… I don't care. The pain is welcome.

Knowing that I healed you. That I helped you, and the night I needed you to help me, you were with her, really left a permanent scar on my heart. I slept on a rug by a butcher shop. Like a stray dog. Mom picked me up the next morning and took me to the hospital. I had frostbite and was near hyperthermic with a concussion and in need of six stitches for my head. And you were too busy with her to notice or care.

Love, Sabrina

I throw the paper down and squeeze my eyes shut. He was so bad, when it came down to it he never really cared. "Brina?" Sam's voice carries through the living space. He rubs his eyes and stretches up. I watch his muscles constrict and relax.

"I just… couldn't sleep," I answer.

"Why are you reading those?" I stare at the paper in my hand.

"I don't remember," I sigh. I don't; I really don't understand why.

"You'll throw them away tomorrow," he says.

"But—"

"No. You wrote those to someone who was supposed to be dead. He doesn't deserve them. He never did." I nod and slip the letter back easily. I slide off the couch and he wraps his arm around me, leading me into the bedroom. Broome curls up between us and I smile softly.

"I love you, Bri."

"I love you too, Sam."

Chapter Ten

The morning is cold. I curl up into the comforter shivering against it. Sam is missing from the bed. I stand up and as soon as I do my stomach lurches. I run to the bathroom before spilling last night's dinner into the toilet. Pizza is not as good coming back up. Another wave passes and I breathe deeply, but it's no use.

"You okay?" Sam finally makes his presence known, dropping behind me.

"Maybe the pizza?" I say, leaning into him. He reaches under the sink and hands me a washcloth. I wipe my mouth and he helps me stand. I grab my toothbrush and start brushing as hard as possible. I bend down and rinse. "Where were you at?" I ask.

"Come on." His smile is huge. He moves behind me and covers my eyes. I walk slowly in front, letting him guide me. We stop and I can feel the warmth of the fireplace.

"Three, two, one." He moves his hands and I feel myself light up. The whole house is covered in Christmas decorations. He sat up a tree with ornaments and garlands all neat beside it.

"I thought we could decorate it together." I twist around and jump onto him.

"Thank you," I whisper.

He carries me over to the tree and we start placing everything on it. It's fresh, making it smell like pine.

"When does your family get in?" he asks.

"Mom said they should land around one," I say.

"Is the guest room set up?"

"Yes, I did that while you were at work yesterday."

"How are we going to fit them all exactly?"

"Deryl is going to get a hotel for them, mom is staying here. Let's just hope Lola and Broome get along" I laugh. He kisses the side of my head, and walks away into the guest bathroom.

"We need to get her stuff!" he calls. I shake my head. Sam is such a good host, but my mother will have everything she needs.

"I can go out. Go grab a couple presents," I answer. He emerges and pulls out his wallet, handing me his card.

"Don't put us into poverty." I slap his chest. We laugh and kiss before I head to the bedroom. I pull on some gray sweatpants over my shorts and my black snow boots. My shirt is white and thin so I decide to steal Sam's thick jacket, putting on a beanie. I run out the door. I knock on Vic's as soon as I reach it and she answers moments later. Of course she's all dolled up and sipping coffee.

"Let's go shopping," I say, and without hesitation she's right next to me entering the elevator.

"So...," she starts as we head towards the closest shopping center.

"So."

"How are you guys doing?" she asks.

"You see us every Saturday," I laugh.

"A lot can change in four days." She shrugs.

"Well, nothing has." She nods and we enter the center.

"What are we getting?" I shrug and she leads us in and out of stores. Eventually, I have presents for everyone. We start down the street towards our building, the wind whips around us. Stinging my skin with every lash.

"Why did we walk?" Vic groans. I laugh at her and her heeled boots. We finally enter the warm lobby and she sighs.

"Brina!" My eyes dart to the couches and Alyssa bolts to me. All the bags drop as she whips me up into a strong hug.

"Why are you here? What about your parents?" I question as she finally releases me.

"Ah they went to Hawaii," she says, waving me off. We gather the discarded bags and all enter the elevator. Vic grabs Lyssa's duffel bag and she smiles at her.

"Your hair is so pretty," Alyssa giggles.

"Thank you, yours is too." Lyssa shrugs at that response. Sam greets us all and helps to unpack everything. I rush away the presents and Vic says goodbye before returning to her own abode.

"Sammy Sam," Alyssa is already doing her duty of annoying the fuck out of him. He looks at me with pleading eyes and all I can do is laugh at both of them. I walk into the living room, and as soon as I sit down, Sam throws Alyssa over the couch and she lands right on me. She cries as her wrist bends at an awkward angle.

"Holy shit!" Sam exhales and runs over.

She holds it close to her chest. "I didn't mean to call you Samantha," she gasps and I laugh a little, helping her lean up.

"I'll warm up the car," Sam says, slipping out the door.

"Let me see it," I say and remove her other hand. It's already discolored and bent in a gross way. She cringes when I touch it.

"I think he owes you for one." She nods and lets out a small laugh.

Sam comes back and I wrap a blanket around her, guiding her down and into his car. My phone starts to ring, "Hello?"

"I'm grabbing a taxi, can you send me your address?" Mom says over the speaker.

"Actually, can you meet us at St. Michaels? Alyssa's already injured herself. She's fine," I say.

Mom sighs. "Yeah, yeah. I'll be there. Deryl is going to the hotel to help Christina get all the kids settled."

"Okay, love you."

"You too, hun," she says and hangs up.

"Mom's gonna meet us there."

"Great," Lyssa says from the front.

"You owe me a kitten," she snarls at Sam.

"I can do that." I can tell he feels bad. Sam is empathetic. He feels deeply for others. I've learned, however, that this is what harms him too. He hides his emotions from anyone he isn't close to, for fear someone will manipulate him. I try to not let Sam see how much I know about him already. I try to let it slide if he gets worked up or upset. I know in reality he doesn't want me to know. At least not the full extent of his emotions.

We pull into the busy ER and I help Lyssa out. We walk up to the nurse's station where she hands us a clipboard and asks us to sit. We find a small couch and all crowd in together. Sam helps her start the forms and I watch the lobby. People are all hanging around, some pacing others sitting on phones. A pregnant lady sits in a wheelchair holding on to a man's shoulder. She smiles at him and rubs her belly, I watch them. In awe of them.

"Help!" a man's voice carries.

"Please help her!" he screams, the strain in his voice makes me stand. I watch him run in. A girl, young looking, maybe twelve, lays in his arms. I step back and gasp. Her body is pale, drained of blood. Blood leaks from her arms as she lays completely lifeless in this poor man's arms. Tears spill from his eyes and he looks exhausted. Doctors and nurses rush over as he drops to his knees. They wrestle her away and lay her flat on her back, a young doctor climbs over her and starts CPR. I hear her ribs crack and I stumble, feeling Sam grab ahold of me.

"Don't watch," he whispers. They try to revive her, but she's long gone. The man lets out a gut-wrenching scream that makes me wince.

"My baby! Not her, not my girl!" He scoops her up and squeezes her tightly. He cries into her hair. All the nurses and doctors bow their heads.

Alyssa is standing now too, forms filled out by her side.

"It feels wrong to give these to the lady now," she mumbles. She has never been good in serious situations, but you can tell she carries a deep sorrow for this.

"Sir, can you let us take her?" a nurse asks, he shakes his head hard. She purses her lips and waves. They place a stretcher behind him. "Just lay back," she says, lightly pushing his shoulder. His cries harden as he does so, holding tightly to her. They position her so she lays right on top of him.

"Not my baby," he cries. They wheel them back into the elevator. Alyssa moves in front of me, walking slowly to the desk. The nurse gives her a bracelet in return for the forms and she joins us as a couple people come to clean up the blood.

Mom comes in eventually, eyeing the mess curiously. I shake my head at her and she nods in an understanding way. We wait in these walls for what feels like forever. Alyssa stares at the male ortho doctor as he holds her hand out.

"This is gonna hurt," he says and quickly snaps it so it's straight. She screams and starts cussing. He only laughs. I lay my head on Sam's shoulder while she gets her wrist wrapped up. The sun has started to dip below the line of buildings and the busy street has calmed slightly. "Go easy on it," he says. Alyssa signs more forms and we finally stand to leave. This is the longest day of my life, minus my work days. Sam practically drags me to the car where Mom has already piled her stuff in. She and I contort in the backseat to fit and I'm asleep as soon as the car starts moving.

Chapter Eleven

The following morning I'm ripped out of bed with another wave of nausea. I power through it and take a hot shower, replacing my Christmas pajamas before joining my family in the living room. I'm thankful Sam has a rather big living space, especially to support Deryl's abundance of children.

"Aunt Bee!" I bend down to embrace them all, at least those who can walk, little Evangeline babbles from her mother's arms. I stand back up and go to hug my brother and sister-in-law.

"You look good, Brina." Deryl smiles. I'm going to assume he's comparing it to any and all Asher experiences. I'll take it. The morning is filled with chatter and loud yells of kids. By evening my head is pounding while we gather around a table to eat. Alyssa scowls at the lack of use in her hand while she tries to scoop chicken into her mouth. Mom and Sam cooked this whole thing. I smile and laugh with them, but it's been a full year since I've known he was alive. Since Mom got this bundle of fluff that's laying under the table waiting on the kits to throw food. Since I met Sam.

"Bri," he whispers. I look over. "Let's get everyone in front of the tree to open gifts," he says and I nod. We organize everyone and we all pass out the presents. Mom brought two trash bags full, of course. The kids excitedly start ripping away and I open my few. I got some makeup, a couple books, and clothing articles. I sit and watch Sam open the few things I got him. Simple things. Alyssa screeches at some exclusive POP figure. When everyone is done, Sam moves in front of my spot on the couch, looking at the books. I watch him, his eyes slowly move to mine and I smile.

"Brina."

"Sam."

"I'm so glad Vic gave me your number." He smiles.

I feel heat creep up my cheeks, tinting them a bright pink. He reaches to the pocket of his Christmas PJ pants, my breath catches in my chest as he reveals a black velvet box. I can't hear a word he is saying. My chest is pumping faster than a NASCAR race. My body is covered in pins and needles. Focus, listen, focus Sabrina.

"You are the only girl that has ever loved me completely and totally. Before you I was convinced I would live the rest of my life alone...." His words blend together. Like a drunk man's confession. "Will you marry me, Sabrina?" I hold my breath for a second, peering around at my eager friends and family. My eyes meet his again and it all washes over me. A mix of emotions, blending together, and crushing me. I know I'm crying, I can't speak. So I nod and collapse into him. He holds us both up while everyone cheers. This feels like it can be right. Like it could be the rest of my life.

The kids all hurry to pile up on the floor of the guest room, excited for Santa to find them and bring them all kinds of things. The air is filled with that feeling, that simple feeling Christmas always brings. The kids all hope Santa will bring them new bikes or fancy toys they have seen on TV. Mom, Deryl, Christina, and Alyssa all excited to both see them open all their new things and get small treats for themselves. Sam has slipped off into a deep sleep, and I move to go to the bathroom.

Tonight has changed my life completely, it's turned me into an actual adult. It set the motion for the rest to pave the way. My alarm snaps me out of it. I turn it off and flip over the pink capped stick. Taking in a deep breath, I can feel it. I can feel the bricks being laid out in front of me. For my new life. And it's all being measured by the sparkly ring on my finger and deep colored + on the screen. And it's not who I always imagined it would be.

I exit the bathroom and walk into the living room, where Deryl is munching on the sugar cookies the kids left. He dumps the milk into the sink and gnaws on a carrot. My brother has only ever wanted to get to be Santa for his kids. When he finally sees me he jumps back.

"Sorry," I whisper. He chuckles and waves me over. I shove the stick into my pocket. Sam and I wore matching pajamas. It was cheesy but whatever. I make my way to him while he begins making Santa prints with my powdered sugar.

"You're growin up, Little B," he says.

"You could say that," I laugh. He focuses on setting up all the gifts, and I grab a small gift bag from the ones we set aside earlier. While Deryl isn't paying attention I throw the test in and shove in tissue paper. I write Sam's name on the front and slip it under the tree.

"What's that?" he asks.

"That's a surprise."

* * *

The kids wake everyone up before the sun even rises the next morning. They are all lit up; smiling and laughing while they jump around and drag everyone into the living room. I push back nausea and let Sam lead me behind the little ones. Deryl lets them explore the wonderland he created while I settle comfortably on the couch. Presents start flying everywhere and I anxiously wait for Deryl to hand Sam his. When he does, he looks at Deryl confused.

"Santa delivers for everyone." He shrugs. Sam takes the bag. Suddenly the fire is too hot; it's boiling my skin. I hold my breath tight, watching him pull out the paper and slowly unwrap it. Everyone else is preoccupied. He stares at it for a long time, too long.

"Holy shit!" he yells excitedly, jumping to his feet. Everyone turns to look. "Holy shit!" he yells again and scoops me off the couch. Tears are streaming down his face soaking the top of my shirt.

"What's going on?" Mom questions, walking over while Sam sits me down. He hands her the stick and she gasps, placing a hand over her mouth. She wraps me up in a hug, "I'm going to be a grandma again!" she cries. I peer over her shoulder and my eyes meet my brother's. He's dumbfounded.

"You're growing up," he mutters.

The morning is filled with tears and laughter. It has been the perfect Christmas. "I'm going to Bev's. I have a present for her," I tell Sam. He kisses me softly and I exit the building quickly. Bev's isn't that far, so I make the awful decision to just walk. The wind strikes my face sharply, slicing through me like a knife. I race across the street and hop around the patches of ice. This winter has been awful weatherwise. Bev's is always open on Christmas for those who need a warm place to go. Bev works all alone, anyone who wants to come in is allowed. I walk through the doors and let the warm air wash over me. I unwrap my scarf and head into the back.

There's only a couple people lingering in the café, most of which appear to be homeless. "Bev," I call softly.

"In here, love," she returns.

I walk back in between dry stock and make my way to her baking table, adjusting her present in my hands. I look up and immediately am hit. "You." The word leaves my lips before I can catch it. He stands there, so sure of himself. She does the same, by his side. I grip the handle of the bag, hard. Different cake slices lay in front of them and she has a fork dug in Bev's amazing dark chocolate espresso cake. "I was just doing a tasting for an upcoming wedding. What can I do for ya dear?" she says, wiping her hands on her apron. Our eyes stay locked while I step to Bev and hand her the gift. I break away to hug Bev.

"Merry Christmas," I say to her. She smiles and places the bag on a rolling shelf. She pulls out the sprinkle set I bought her followed by the narrow box. She turns to face me. I can see Asher watching her too. She lifts the lid and gasps, pulling out the same stick that has been passed around all day. I felt it, the small smile settle on my lips. Asher coughs hard and rushes from the room. His fiancée watches him and huffs.

"He has been so antsy since we got to New York," she says. She doesn't need to explain any of it to me. Why in the hell would he choose to come here for his wedding. He knows I live here. "My daddy will be here soon, though," she smiles at Bev. Completely ignoring my presence.

"How far along?" Bev asks.

"I'm not sure yet," I answer. The girl is clearly discouraged by this. "This will be my Ashey's first time meeting my dad," she pipes in.

"Cool," I say flatly.

"Baby," a man sings, while Bev hands me back my test.

"Mr. Foster." Bev smiles. I turn to look and my eyes meet my own. This is nothing like the feeling of seeing Asher. I step back, closer to Bev. Begging this old lady for protection; don't let him get me.

"Daddy!" she runs over and wraps him in a hug. "I'm so glad you could make it." She sounds like a squeak toy, or no, like Odeal from the Barbie version of Swan Lake. He hugs her tight and pulls her back to look her over.

"I wouldn't miss it. Your mom is coming. She's looking at all those beautiful cakes out front." *Mom? Daddy?* It finally settles, the realization.

"I should go," I whisper to Bev. She nods and I go to leave while the girl—Danielle, I think—and Bev return to the cakes. I step towards the door, but he stops me. A chill cuts down my spine, the all-too-familiar feeling of fear deep in me.

"Not even going to say hi?" He smirks. I stare at the tips of my boots.

"I have nothing to say." I look up at him "Daddy." I shove past him and he wraps his hand around my shoulder spinning me so my back lays flat against the wall. "Don't," I choke out. Danielle and Bev are hidden behind shelves, out of sight.

"You're still a snarky bitch aren't you?" His voice rattles me to the bone.

"Get your hands off of me, Chris," I manage to say.

"Why?" he steps closer. Suddenly I'm sixteen again....

His hands are on each side of my head, pinning me against the door of my bedroom. Alcohol soaks his crisp button-up and his tie dangles.

"Dad, please," I beg. He doesn't listen, and pushes down the band of my sleep shorts anyway.

"Get off!" I push him hard. He steps back and I bolt. I slip at the counter and try to catch myself but instead arms wrap around me. Don't be—oh. Asher stares at me, his eyes red rimmed. He pulls me upright, hands remaining on my hips. He sniffles and looks down.

"I'm so sorry," he says. I consider him for a moment. I remember when he gave me that necklace. When he kissed me, in the pouring rain. When he crawled through my window, sped down the midnight streets, bought me a doughnut for my birthday. "Bye."

Chapter Twelve

I called Sam to pick me up and as soon as I stepped through the door, I crashed into my mom's arms. I told her everything. She holds me still, shocked. Dad had a whole other life, a whole other family. And yet he still treated us like shit. Me, like shit. The way he hugged her today, that was all I have ever wanted. Sam sits at my feet with Deryl. Sam has his hand on my side and Deryl is holding my hand tight. Mom runs her hands through my hair, even though she, too, is crying. I feel like I'm drowning in this feeling. This fear of him being back. The hurt of him having them, and the utter most intense feeling of betrayal on Asher's end. To me and my family. I stay here for hours. Until my eyes grow heavy and I slip off to sleep.

Sam –

I trace small circles on her belly under her hoodie. Her mom hasn't stopped crying yet, silent tears fall and splash on Sabrina's head. Deryl looks like he could kill someone. "Can one of you tell me what happened? What was she talking about?" I ask gently.

Deryl cringes and lays his head on her hand. Anne uses her free hand to wipe her face. "My husband was an evil man to us. He hit me, most of the time. We got together in high school; I got pregnant senior year with Deryl. So we got married, that way we could start working to support our baby. His dad got him an internship at the airport and he worked his way up. Eventually Sabrina was born too. I had two babies to take care of. I worked every single weekend to help support our family.

I knew he was cheating. Before Sabrina was born, he was suddenly never home. Always saying he had to work late, but I knew he was lying. There wasn't much for him to do there at that time. But I knew I couldn't leave. And when I was in the hospital staring at my beautiful baby girl while her brother held her I didn't care anymore. I figured that if I could make it, at least until they moved out, they wouldn't be hurt as bad. I wanted them to grow up with a dad. To have that figure in their lives. But as Sabrina got older and Asher was around more and more Chris was always mad at her. She tried too hard for him. All she ever wanted was for her daddy to love her. She worked so hard to be what she thought he wanted. I didn't know what to do the first time he hit her. I threw myself in front of her whenever. But I was gone when he was home a lot to maintain our financial stability.

I screamed at him. I tried to make him leave more than once. Then he found out that she and Asher had sex. That he was sneaking in at night to see her. He—" She chokes for a second and Deryl clenches his jaw. "He started to hurt her. More. In a different way. I remember when she collapsed in the kitchen. He didn't move to help her. Asher picked her up and we went to the hospital. She was pregnant. Seventeen. She was only seventeen. I remember Deryl hit Asher and they had to break them apart. Eight weeks is what the doctor said. But Asher was away at a football camp. The realization hit me like a truck. I stomped to the waiting room. I screamed at him at the top of my lungs. Deryl eventually pieced it together too. When he tried to get to her room, we stood in a line. Alyssa, Deryl, Asher, Asher's brother, and me. We stood up to him. We blocked him and wouldn't even let him see her. I was so disgusted."

I try to let all of this information sink in. Let it resonate. "What happened to the baby?" I manage to ask. She shakes her head and Deryl looks up to me. Tears running down his face now too.

"Asher was over. They were watching a movie. Asher got a text from some girl and she got upset. She made him leave and Dad showed up. Neither of us were home. Asher was supposed to be with her. To protect her. Dad beat her to a pulp. Until the kitchen was full of blood. When I got home, she was curled in a ball. It was the most sickening scene. She was holding on to her little belly. She let out this heart-stopping scream. I felt it to my core. And I just held her. That's all I could do. I was covered in her blood. My baby sister and her baby."

Bile rises in my throat, suddenly all I can feel is the food I ate at the beginning of the day. "It's a lot to take in, we know," Anne sighs. I look at Sabrina. Her hair is a mix of blonde and brown now. Her face is completely pale, eyes red and swollen. Pieces of stray hairs stick to her face. My hand moves over her stomach. It's usually completely flat, but now there's a small bulge around her abdomen. My baby is there, growing inside this wonderful woman.

I can't let that man hurt her or these people that have become such important members of my life. My family has never been there for me. I watched Mom shoot up every night and Dad drank away his liver. Sabrina and the Foster family are my life now. I actually am considering taking her name when we get married. She moans and twists her body away from my touch. Her eyes slowly peel open. They look sore. My heart aches thinking about how much pain she must be in.

"What happened?" she asks with a gravelly voice. Deryl stands and moves towards the guest room before she sees his tears.

"It's okay my love," her mom says. She slowly sits up and wipes her face.

"I—" She stops and swallows. "I want to shower," she says looking at me.

"Stay here," I say and stand. My legs are sore from sitting on the floor for so long, but I ignore the ache while I head to our bathroom. I turn the water on as hot as I can stand it and get her towels and such ready before heading back to the living room. She is hunched over now with her mom rubbing her back. There is some vomit on the hardwood, not much though considering she's barely eaten.

"I'll clean it up," her mom whispers. I nod and kneel in front of her.

"You ready?" She nods. I try to help her up, but her legs shake under her so I just scoop her up and carry her into the bathroom. She sits on the toilet while I pull her clothes off. I use some trimming scissors to cut out her hair tie, fearful of it hurting her. "Up you go," I say and pull her up. She stays leaning against me.

"My head hurts so bad," she mutters and buries her face in my chest. I can feel her crying again. I shush her and rub her back, realizing she won't stand in the shower by herself. I pull off my jeans and shirt, so I'm down to my boxers and tank top. We get in and I begin to wash her hair. Using way too much conditioner but I fear she won't get a hairbrush through it in the morning. I twist her around and let the water rinse off her face. After we are done I help her out and wrap her in towels before drying off myself and switching my boxers while she sits on the bed.

I put her in some pajama shorts and one of my shirts before tucking her into bed with some Advil. I put on another shirt and some basketball shorts before cleaning up the dirty clothes and heading into the living room. The vomit is clean and Deryl now sits on the couch with Christina. Baby Evangeline lays on Chrissy's chest sleeping.

"How is she?" Anne asks.

"She's asleep now. Her head hurts, is what she told me." Anne nods and finishes washing the dishes.

"I'm selling my house," she tells me. "I found an apartment near here. I want to be here for you and Sabrina. Help with the baby when it comes," she tells me.

"You don't have to—"

"I want to. That house is too big for me. Way to many bad memories." She waves me off.

"Sabrina will love that."

"I know, plus they allow pets." She laughs looking down at Lola and Broome cuddling in the corner of the kitchen. Sabrina loves that cat that's for sure. "Deryl moving to the big city too?" I ask, swinging to face the living room. "Nah, we just live in Pennsylvania. It's not that far," Deryl says from the couch.

"Anne, that couch turns into a bed if you're sick of sleeping in the guestroom," I tell her.

"You should have told Alyssa that," Deryl groans. I walk toward the guest room door. All the kids are sleeping on their mattresses and Alyssa is in the center of the big bed. I laugh and walk to the couch.

"Up," I say. Chrissy stands keeping Eve asleep and Deryl helps guide them aside. I unfold the bed and get the mattress pad and sheets from the hall closet. When the bed has been made up, I lift Alyssa out of Deryl and Chrissy's bed and allow them to get some sleep. Anne has already pulled back the covers. When Alyssa is tucked in, Anne moves next to her and they are both snoring with the dog and cat before I even reach my bedroom door. Deryl's family heads home tomorrow. It's definitely going to be quiet around here without them all. I close our bedroom door lightly and try hard not to wake up Sabrina as I pull the covers over myself.

My body is facing Sabrina's. She is the most beautiful woman I have ever laid eyes on. I know she deeply cared for someone before me. Whoever the Asher guy was has clearly made an impression on everyone in this family. Maybe I can meet him someday. Although from some of the things I've heard I can't promise not to break his nose. Sabrina didn't deserve what he or her dad put her through.

Chapter Thirteen

Sabrina-

It's been a week since Deryl left. The apartment feels empty, but Mom and Alyssa are sticking around. Mom for good now. Lyssa wants to stay until I have the baby. She brought her work computer and has set up at the bar with her notebooks and pencils etc. I don't mind, neither does Sam. Having more people around makes me feel safe. As opposed to Sam going to work and me sitting alone hoping Chris won't show up. Sam won't tell me everything that happened when I got home from that day. It's all foggy. I just remember that he took care of me. That was all I could ask for.

I sit on the couch watching TV while Mom cleans up the last of the Christmas stuff. Lola lays at my feet while Broome is curled up in my lap. I miss Deryl and the kids, but I really am enjoying this bit of peace. Mom is cleaning the kitchen and Alyssa is snoring from the guest room. As much as I want to show her around the city and see her try to ice skate, the idea of seeing all of them again is traumatizing. Sam says I can't hide out forever. My last bit of classes are supposed to pick up again soon. I know he's right. I can't hide away forever, I just want to feel safe until I can't avoid it anymore. Knowing Chris is walking around New York with his new daughter and my ex is absolute torture to my mind. I can't explain how it feels honestly. It's like an empty feeling down in my core. Almost like when you start new anxiety medicine and need to cry but can't.

I want to be okay with it; with Asher. It's just that this feeling was unexpected and hurtful. Sam is at work, so I take this moment of independence and slip into our room. I close the door quietly and make my way to my nightstand. I dig through papers and random items until my fingers touch the smooth surface I am needing. My knees drag up to my chest and I pull open the box. I know I shouldn't do this, but the need to remember something, anything, is too strong. The letter is in my hands before I can put a second thought into this....

Letter #60

I haven't helped anyone feel better in a long time. Vic was sick this past week and I was trying to help her get up on her feet. She needed a lot of TLC but now she is back to work and on moderation. Helping her reminded me of that time when my parents were out of town and you stayed over. But you slept in the guest bed...

I creep out of my room and open the door to Asher. I find his clothes and pile them in the hall, searching for his jeans so I can wash them. After a few frustrating minutes, I look at him and see him lying on his stomach facing away from me, jeans still on. I let out a puff of air and make my way to him, "Asher," I whisper and try to shake him. He makes no motion to let me know my attempt worked. So I tried a few more times, nothing. Eventually, I just climb onto him and straddle his back. "Ash wake up, I need to wash your clothes." He finally groans, letting me know he heard me, so I roll to the edge of the bed. He pulls off this belt and hands me his pants. "I'm gonna wash these. Do you need anything?" I ask him.

"My back is hurting," he answers and I nod, exiting the room. I toss the clothes into the laundry shoot and hurry downstairs to start the washer. My dad has muscle spasms so I know he has an ointment here somewhere that might help with his pains. I rummage through our medicine cabinet until I find the metal tube and hurry back to his room. I know he isn't back asleep, but he lies perfectly still. I crawl back onto him and lift his white T-shirt up towards his shoulders, I squirt some onto his lower back and he groans in response.

"Sorry," I mutter and begin rubbing it into his skin. I can almost feel the tension from him release beneath me. My fingers trace over the stretch marks that create tiger stripes down his back. I stare at the red lines I left the previous night. Nothing will happen from this little massage session and I know this, but I can feel the deep set emotions. The skin beneath me belongs to something

I so desperately want to be mine. That day was amazing; we cooked dinner and watched movies before you had to go home.
I miss you… I'm sorry.
Love, Sabrina.

My throat is tight and closed off as snot and tears fall from my face, soaking the paper in my hands. I hold it close to my chest as hard as possible, trying to consume the feeling of joy I had while writing it. Asher always let me believe he loved me, even if he didn't. I know deep down he cared, but I will never know if there was any type of love there. I was the girl from his childhood who he was required to care for. Asher was my fairy tale. He made me feel like a girl in a movie. He spun me around and helped me with my schoolwork. He made sure I was happy as best he could. No matter what my dad was doing, he was there to heal my heart. But… in the end he just ended up hurting me worse than Dad ever could. He made me feel loved unlike I ever did with Dad, therefore, when he did the things he did the hurt was way worse. They hurt worse because I expected more from him. I expected that happily ever after. I guess it was my fault for ever expecting anything.

The tears flow freely and I give in to the heavy feeling that cascades over me. I lay down on the rug and curl up into a ball, the paper still pressed to my chest. There's a fog of cold covering the floor, and I let it hurt. For a minute I let myself hurt over Asher Dean. I haven't let it hurt since I mourned his death, I haven't let it hurt since that night in my kitchen. When my body was full of shards of broken glass and the small litters of bruises he pressed into me. I haven't felt this pain in full, and now suddenly it's consuming me. I want to get up, I want to toss this page aside and feel okay, but I can't. Maybe I know I need this for a minute longer.

When the tears dry up and my chest relaxes I know someone is here with me. I sit up slowly, muscles tight and sore. Sam is just sitting on the edge of the bed, my box beside him. He doesn't move, just stares at a black TV. Sam, sweet Sam. He is so good and I know I shouldn't hurt over Asher at all. I know I should be more concerned with my father's presence or anything else. I pull myself up onto the bed, feeling the warmth of the blankets beneath me as I slide over to Sam. I sit up on my knees and place a hand on his shoulder. He flinches but doesn't look towards me.

"Do you love me, Sabrina?" His words are hard.

"Yes." My throat hurts. "I love you Sam."

"Then why am I not enough for you?"

"That's not true Sam. You are enough."

"I'm enough?" He finally looks at me, but I wish he hadn't. It would be so much easier if he hadn't.

"Sam—"

"No matter how much better I am than him, you continue to want his love again. He never loved you. From what I have gathered from not only you but your family? That boy has not earned a single tear you are spilling for him. I have been there for you. I held you when you cried, I rushed to your side when you called, I held your damn body up in the shower while you were so out of it you couldn't even speak. I have earned you, Sabrina. I deserve you.

"Him and his new family couldn't care less about you. We, here in this apartment, we care. I thought you were better than some pathetic schoolgirl moping over some old crush. We are having a child for Christ's sakes. And he has done all this before, but you're lying to yourself that he will ever be there for you. You're lying on the floor of our apartment, crying over some asshole. Let him go. Let him go or let me go, because I know I am better than this. Better than just some back-up plan in your sad story." Sam walks out of the room and slams the door behind him. I peer over at the edge of our bed. At the box of memories. I know everything Sam said was true. There's no but to the fact either; I know he's right. He is always right. Am I really pathetic enough to let the past ruin the future? I leap off of the bed and hurry out the door, but Sam is already gone.

"He will be back, my love," my mom says.

"I know; he's Sam."

Mom smiles softly and I return it best I can. I can't believe I let him leave, I should have stopped him. There are so many things that are up in the air right now and I don't want Sam and me to be one of them. The rest of the evening I sit on the couch staring at the TV. Alyssa has tried to cheer me up, but I will feel better only when Sam comes home. Mom makes dinner and hands me a plate and drink. However, I have no appetite. I stare at the pasta bake and feel my stomach growl, pleading with me to take a bite. Has Sam had dinner? It's gotten dark and snow is blowing hard against the windows. Alyssa lights a fire to warm up the place, yet I sit and wait.

The two move around me wrapping up routines, but I stay still, staring at the dancing fire. I'm broken out of my gaze by a knock. I jump up, expecting Sam to have just forgotten his keys. I stumble back when I see a nearly frozen Asher standing there. He looks at me for a long while, eyes travel down to my stomach and back up to my face. He hands me an envelope and walks away. I step to the doorframe and watch as he goes down the elevator. The envelope is cream colored and sealed with a gold wax rose. I peel it up and read through the formal printed invitation

"You're invited to the union of Asher Dean and Danielle Foster… blah blah blah. Bri, please come. Your dad won't even look at you. I promise. I want you there more than anything. I miss you. Love, Ash." I push my head back into the doorframe and stare up at the cracked hall ceiling. Water drips on Vic's side, creating a large gray spot down the wall. The elevator dings and Sam steps out shaking snow from his hair. I drop the letter and run to him, jumping onto him. His body is cold, he reluctantly wraps his arms around me and eases into me.

"I love you," I whisper.

* * *

Would you believe it if I told you Sam still isn't talking to me? Only when necessary which isn't a great feeling. Today we have a gender reveal mom planned and Asher's wedding is in a week; I still haven't decided if I'm going to go. Nor if I'm going to ask Sam to come. Today is supposed to be a happy day for us, and my fiancé I are supposed to love one another. We know nothing about our baby. Mom has been keeping all the information. All I know is there is nothing to worry about.

Enjoy this moment when we find out if we are having a son or daughter. The theme is dumb in my opinion, but Mom was excited about it. She moved into an empty complex downstairs about three weeks ago and has kept all of the decorations away from me. I, however, don't mind the presence of donuts. There is a chance I will eat all of them myself. We have a guessing raffle, boys bring diapers and girls wipes. It's an easy way to stock up. The nursery is painted gray, and has random items scattered about. At least after this I can start buying clothes that aren't basic, and decorations. We have a white crib with matching dresser, in-table, etc.

I stare at myself in the floor-length mirror we have placed in the hall. The dress Lyss and Vic shoved me in hugs onto me and defines the little bump I have developed. It's tie-dyed pink and blue with white mostly covering it. My hair is down and curled and Alyssa forced me to put on at least a bit of makeup. The weather is still rather cool. It won't be too unpleasant at the park today, which is a relief.

"You look pretty," Sam says, leaning in our doorway. I look at him through the mirror. He has on a plain white polo and some dark blue jeans. Sam hasn't spoken to me, and he just did. I smile and bite back tears that threaten to ruin Alyssa's masterpiece.

"You think?" I ask and turn to look at him.

"You're always pretty, Sabrina."

"You're not so bad yourself," I laugh and a small smile lingers on him.

"It's time to go, are you ready?" I nod and step towards him. I want him to touch me. That's all I want at this moment. On this day. But… he doesn't. He walks past me and goes to put on his shoes. I look up and will myself not to cry. I can't cry today, this day is for jellybean.

We head towards the park, following Vic and Matt. This will probably be the most awkward party ever. Sam opens the door for me and grabs my hand to help me out of the car, this is all he does. The only time I feel his skin on mine is when he is being a gentleman.

"Sabrina!" my nieces and nephews yell and run to hug me, almost knocking me over.

"Whoa! Careful, kids," Deryl says and walks to me. "Hey, Brina." He smiles and I wrap my arms around him. He hugs me tight. It makes me feel slightly better about everything going on. "C'mon," he says and leads me up a little hill to a platform. Everything is decorated in beautiful pastel blues and pinks. A banner with a picture of donut holes VS regular donuts hangs across the top. I giggle a bit at the innuendo, and everyone begins greeting Sam and me. People swarm the food and games Mom has set up. I grab a bunch of breadsticks and donuts and begin eating. Sam sits by me, watching everyone with only a couple donut holes on a plate in front of him. Time goes by slowly until Mom is pulling us over to a small field by the gazebo. She hands Deryl and Matt smoke poppers and places Sam and me in front of a wardrobe tied with white ribbon. It's a beautiful wardrobe, white to match the bedroom.

Sam pulls the end of the ribbon and everyone counts down, "Three, two, one" and we swing the doors open as the poppers go off.

"Two?" I say and look at Mom. Pink and blue smoke pours around us and Mom nods, wiping the tears from her eyes. I light up inside and jump onto Sam. He wraps his arms around me for the first time in weeks, lifting me off the ground and spinning. "Twins!" I squeal as he sets me down. Everyone runs from the gazebo and circles us in hugs. I look over Vickey's shoulder towards the park and see Asher, hands stuffed in his pockets as he stares.

"I wanted him to see," Sam whispers.

Chapter Fourteen

I look at Sam confused, until Ash walks down the hill towards us all. Sam steps through everyone and meets Asher with a handshake. I go to them as well, and Deryl is right behind me. Deryl doesn't seem shocked, though, and I suddenly feel like I'm part of an inside joke.

"Glad you showed," Sam says and Asher nods.

"Can we talk?" he asks me. I look at my brother and Sam and they nod. My shoulders slump and Ash grabs my hand to help me up the hill to an empty bench. I sit and hold my stomach, using my babies for comfort.

"What do you want?" I ask. I try my best to not sound mean.

"To talk. Sam asked me to come and talk to you. He's a good guy for you, Bri."

"I know," I choke on my own words.

"He told me…about the letters you wrote." Ash reaches into a bag beside him and pulls the box out. I'm shocked to see him holding it. All the letters. The tears, the memories, all of it in Asher's hands. Everything was about him.

"I… how did you?"

"Sam gave it to me. I read them, all of them. And I won't lie, it hurts. It hurt to see and understand how bad I actually hurt you. I was a coward, Sabrina. I didn't want you to think that I didn't love you, but when you went off to school, I knew I needed to cut ties. We have always bounced off of each other. No matter how much it hurt, we always came together and it was killing us. Being together felt… expected. If that makes sense. It felt like everyone only wanted us to be together. I didn't want that, though. I love you, Sabrina, and I want you there when I reach those milestones. Sam reached out, found me on Facebook of all places. I know you, and I know you need closure. I want you to live your life, with him, with your babies. I want you to let go of what we were, we both need to. I read them, I read them all." He looks at my belly and smiles. I suddenly know what we need to do. I grab the box from Asher and look down the hill. The sun is starting to set, perfect timing.

"Sabrina?" Asher stands behind me, and I grab his hand pulling him down the hill. "Be careful," he laughs and I just keep going. Everyone has started leaving, only the important ones remain. "We burn them" I say, out of breath. Mom, Deryl, Lyss, Sam, everyone, they all look at me like I've lost my mind. "Get some sticks and stuff, please" I say and they stumble around searching. I open the box and sift through them, pulling out the one I wanted. There's a small stack of sticks in the little firepit by the gazebo now, Matt hands Sam a lighter and he lights it. The flames dance like they do at home. I unfold the letter and begin reading.

"One more kiss and I'll go. I promise you; you'll never have to hear my voice again. Never see me again. I can't promise not to watch your life in pictures. Not to stare into the river of your brown eyes or swim in the depths of indentions of your cheek, or color roses with the shade of your lips. Your smile bites my heart in one of the most painful depths of despair I have ever sunken into. You, my love. You hurt me more than I will ever be able to understand. I Can't help but feel like in a way this happened for a reason. Happened because I needed you gone. I just never imagined this would be how you went. You, Asher, you will always have my heart in a way no one can compare. And now I say goodbye…."

Sam holds my shoulders and I turn to Asher. "Goodbye to the memories," I say to him and stand up on my toes to kiss his cheeks.

"Goodbye to the letters to him," Sam says and we all throw them into the flames. The paper coils and turns into dust. We watch as it floats up into the air piece by piece.

Epilogue

"One more push," Sam whispers and I nod. I'm beyond exhausted at this point and need her here. Blake cries from his bassinet as nurses tend to him. I push one last time and my scream blends with that of our daughter's. I fall back into the bed and Sam kisses my head.

"Don't, I'm sweaty," I sigh.

"You're beautiful." I smile and look over to where the babies are.

"Okay, little man is comin'," the nurse says and carries him over. Sam helps me put the bed up more and I reach for my son. He stares up at me through clouded eyes.

"Hi," I whisper, "I'm your mama." a tear drops from my eye and onto his cheek making him flinch.

"Here comes the baby girl," another nurse says. I watch Sam scoop her up timidly. She kicks her legs and he sits down next to me.

"Let me see," I say eagerly and he carefully holds her towards me. I think we made the prettiest babies in the world. Sam and I landed on the names Blake Asher and Briar Alyssa-Anne. Believe it or not, giving Blake the middle name Asher was Sam's idea. Time passes by and soon the door bursts open and everyone spills in ready to meet our babies. Asher and Danni are dressed up in rehearsal dinner outfits and I immediately feel bad for ruining their night.

"Oh my, they are gorgeous, you guys!" my mom gushes and takes Briar from Sam. Deryl sits by me and begins playing with Blake's hand while he sleeps soundly against me.

"Let me see." Ash says and leans over Deryl.

"What are their names?" Lyssa asks, playing with my daughter's hands. "Blake Asher and Briar Alyssa-Anne." I smile and watch faces light up with joy. "Ahh, let me see my goddaughter!" Lyssa screeches and scoops her from my mom.

"Why did you guys?" Asher asks while Deryl hands Blake to him.

"These babies are the future of us," Sam tells him. "Of Sabrina, and I know how much you mean to her, Asher. I know how much the memories meant." They shake hands and I watch my babies be passed around and held. Watching Asher, I know now that this is how it was meant to be. As much as I may miss him, as I did miss him, Asher was never meant to be my endgame; he was just meant to cheer me on. A built-in best friend, and if we had realized this ahead of time we would have never been forced to go through the things we did.

Letters to Him

Official Playlist

Track one: *Paradise* by Cold Play
Track two: *That Girl* by Kenzie Cait
Track three: *They Don't Know About Us* by 1D
Track four: *Time of Our Lives* by Tyrone Wells
Track five: *Haunted* by Taylor Swift
Track six: *Drunk Text Me* by Lexi Jayde
Track seven: *Every Little Thing* by Carly Pierce
Track eight: *Like That* by Bea Miller
Track nine: *A Soulmate Who Wasn't Meant to Be* by Jess Benko
Track ten: *False Confidence* by Noah Kahan
Track eleven: *Compass* by Lady A
Track twelve: *Sparks Fly* by Taylor Swift